PANTHERS' P

Impulse 1

Zara Chase

MENAGE EVERLASTING

Siren Publishing, Inc.
www.SirenPublishing.com

A SIREN PUBLISHING BOOK
IMPRINT: Ménage Everlasting

PANTHERS' PLEASURE
Copyright © 2013 by Zara Chase

ISBN: 978-1-62242-381-1

First Printing: February 2013

Cover design by Les Byerley
All art and logo copyright © 2013 by Siren Publishing, Inc.

Printed in the U.S.A.

PUBLISHER
Siren Publishing, Inc.
www.SirenPublishing.com

PANTHERS' PLEASURE

Impulse 1

ZARA CHASE
Copyright © 2013

Chapter One

Chantal consulted the map spread across her lap as she waited for the signal to change. A GPS in her ancient car would be nice, navigation not being her strong point. A better car wouldn't go amiss, come to that.

"It should be right about here somewhere," she said aloud, with more conviction than she felt.

She moved forward when the light turned green and felt mildly euphoric when she came to a waterside bar with a brightly painted sign swinging in the breeze.

"The Cat's Whiskers," she said, peering through the windshield to make sure she was at the right place and punching the air. "Yes!"

She pulled her ten-year-old Jeep Wrangler into the vacant lot and cut the engine. It was eleven in the morning and the place appeared deserted. That didn't seem too hopeful. From what she'd seen of Impulse so far it was a quiet town, but surely waterside bars attracted the breakfast crowd? She ought to have known that a temporary job opening up just when and where she happened to need one was too good to be true. This place didn't need help, it needed a complete makeover, or at the very least a crash course on how to attract local trade. And you didn't do that by having the doors closed at eleven on a Friday morning.

Chantal climbed from her car and grabbed her purse from the back seat. She was here now so she might as well see if the place really did need bar staff. Accommodation was supposed to go with the job and that's what had attracted her when she saw the ad on a corkboard at the gas station. Strange place to advertise. Why not use an agency, or at the very least, the "Help Wanted" column in the local paper? She had no way of knowing how old that corkboard ad actually was, but the cute guy behind the counter said it was recent. When she'd asked about it, he'd looked at her in an intense way that made Chantal feel as though he could see right inside her head. Then he nodded as though he liked what he saw and told her she'd suit the vacancy just fine.

Chantal paused as she walked across the lot, aware of a sudden tightness in her chest and difficulty getting enough air into her lungs. She paused, giving herself a moment to recover, wondering if she was coming down with something. The air felt thin, like she was at a high altitude, and yet she was right at sea level. Putting the anomaly down to a combination of tiredness, nerves, and stress, she carried on toward the bar and tried the front door.

It was unlocked so presumably they *were* open. It was hard to tell. She found herself in a gloomy, unlit walkway that led to a surprisingly large *L*-shaped bar. All the shutters were closed, but she guessed that when opened there would be spectacular views of the Intracoastal Waterway immediately beyond. There was a deserted restaurant to the left of the bar that could comfortably seat fifty diners. She poked her head around the door, just in case there was someone about and she'd not seen them.

Not having any luck, Chantal retraced her steps. She thought she'd seen a door further back that might have led to an office. She tapped on it but got no answer.

"Figures," she said, rolling her eyes. "This place is a frigging ghost town."

A noise behind her made her almost jump out of her skin. She spun on her heel and almost collided with a man—no, not a man, a god, she amended, taking quick stock of the hunk who she hadn't heard approaching. No one walked without making any noise at all, did they? It wasn't natural, but then nor was he, and as Chantal's eyes adjusted to the gloom she was unable to suppress a gasp of approval. He was *the* most amazing-looking man she'd ever seen. At least six foot two, he had a lean, fit body and muscles that rippled like running water when he moved his arms. Dressed in tight-fitting black jeans and a black vest that sculpted his body, he attracted Chantal in a way that transcended his glamorous appearance. It was almost as though she was drawn toward him by a force greater than her own will and she found it was impossible to look away.

Her unnamed companion had hair the color of rich dark chocolate, long, smooth, and sleek. She was filled with the desire to reach up to run her fingers through it. What the hell had gotten into her? Chantal shook her head, striving to locate her common sense, which had chosen a most inconvenient time to take a vacation.

Unable to get a grip, she continued to gawp at the man like she'd never seen a hunk before. Well, in her own defense, she hadn't, at least not one that came close to measuring up to this rare specimen of male beauty. She looked into eyes so intensely blue that they made her think of a fresh mountain stream on a summer's day, tempting her to dive right on in. They didn't blink and, as at the gas station, she felt as though the man had the ability to see inside her head and read her thoughts. It ought to have freaked her out. Instead she felt comfortable being held in the elusive warmth of an all-encompassing gaze that appeared to miss little.

Hell if Chantal knew what was going on. All she did know was that the atmosphere radiated with a tingling exhilaration that made it impossible for her to break eye contact with the man. Some ethereal influence outside of her understanding obligated her to lock gazes with him, even as her body reacted in an entirely predictable way. Chantal had been a self-imposed man-free zone for several months and her feminine needs were letting her know they were tired of being neglected.

Turbulent heat washed through her as she withstood the hunk's scrutiny. Color invaded her face and she felt her nipples harden as time stood still and they continued to appraise one another in electrifying silence. Her pussy was leaking like a drain, damn it, simply because he looked at her as though he wanted to eat her alive. It was too humiliating for words to be so damned predictable. The thought that all women must react to the guy in the same manner gave her the strength to break a silence that felt as though it had gone on forever, even though it couldn't have lasted for more than a few tension-filled seconds.

"I'm…er, looking for Rafe Landon," she said, her voice sounding husky and most unlike her own.

"Come in, Chantal," he said, opening the door to the office and standing aside to let her pass through it first. "I'm Rafe. We've been expecting you. Come on up."

Chantal's feet remained rooted to the spot. "How come you know my name?" she asked suspiciously.

This was beyond spooky. She didn't care how good looking he was, or how well-mannered in opening the door for her, she wasn't entering that room alone with him until she got an explanation.

"Zale at the gas station mentioned you'd seen our ad."

"I didn't tell Zale my name."

"Presumably you gave him your credit card." She nodded reluctantly. "Well, there you are then. And Zale gave you directions here—"

"And then phoned you to say to expect me?"

Rafe appeared to find that suggestion amusing, his lazy smile revealing very white, very even teeth. "Something like that."

She frowned. "Why would he do that?"

"It's a small town. We look out for each other." He shrugged. "That's what neighbors do."

"Evidently."

He was still holding the door for her. She hesitated for a moment longer, weighing her options. The way people communicated in Impulse might be weird, but she didn't feel threatened by it, or by Rafe Landon. Besides, she needed to find work and her options were kinda limited in that respect. Shrugging, she walked through the door. Rafe led the way, giving her a good opportunity to check out his butt as he ascended a small flight of stairs. Hell, he was hot! But even the sight of those long legs and that gorgeous ass couldn't detract from the way he moved, all lithe muscle and graceful coordination, almost as though his feet didn't touch the stairs. Talking of feet, she noticed he was barefoot. She guessed shoes were probably superfluous if you could move like that. He had the balance and poise of a dancer but possessed a not entirely civilized aura that marked him as unquestionably male.

"Here we are." He turned toward her as they reached the top of the stairs, a knowing smile flirting with his lips. Once again she got the impression that he knew what she'd been thinking. "We'll be more comfortable in here."

Well, that makes one of us! He ushered her into a living room with a vaulted ceiling, wide, exposed wooden beams stretching high above her head. The room was furnished with overstuffed sofas, low occasional tables, floor-to-ceiling bookshelves, and lots of thick rugs covered the board floor. Blinds almost completely kept the sun from infiltrating the full-length windows, allowing just a glimpse of the water beyond them.

"There's no need to shout."

Startled, Chantal looked for the source of that voice. Rafe hadn't spoken, and as far as she was aware, there was no one else about who could have shouted anything. Another door opened and Chantal was almost blown away by the sight of another unworldly hunk. He was rubbing the sleep from his eyes, making it obvious that he'd just gotten out of bed. He wore a pair of tight-fitting jeans and nothing else, not even any shoes. His muscular chest was peppered with hair as black as that on his head. It narrowed to a thin line down the middle of his torso and disappeared below the waistband of his jeans. Chantal shook her head to dispel images of tracing it to its base. Judging by the bulge in the front of his jeans, that base would be well worth exploring. Christ, she needed to get laid! She now had good reason to know that celibacy wasn't all it was cracked up to be.

When she looked more closely, she noticed this guy had a series of fine white lines crisscrossing his torso. They were almost like operation scars, except they were too fine for that. She wondered what could have caused them. An allergy, perhaps?

Like Rafe, this guy's hair was also long, sleek, and smooth as silk. Pecs bulged as he lifted his hands to his eyes—eyes that were also piercingly blue and which widened in evident approval when they came to rest on Chantal.

"She's here," he said to Rafe.

"That's what I was trying to tell you."

Chantal shook her head, completely unable to figure out how they communicated without words.

"Hello," the second man said. "I'm Vilas Tanner, Rafe's partner. And you must be Chantal."

"Er…yes."

Sparks flew between them as Vilas took her hand. She ignored the dizziness that seeped through her body, wondering instead how he could possibly know her name when it was obvious that he'd only just gotten out of bed. She wondered as well why Vilas had complained about being shouted at when no one had said a word, unless there was someone else up here that Chantal had yet to meet. She doubted it, though. If Vilas had heard shouting, surely she would have, too? These guys really did need a lesson in how to run a decent business.

Sleeping until eleven in the morning was hardly the best way to attract the breakfast trade.

Vilas, still holding her hand, lifted it to his lips. Hell, was he going to kiss it? How old-fashioned was that? Instead, eyes locking with hers, he ran his tongue across the back of it in such a sensuous manner that renewed tremors passed through her. His tongue was very long and surprisingly rough, but the effect it had on her sex-starved body was electrifying.

"Give Chantal her hand back," Rafe said, appearing to find the situation amusing.

"Must I?"

But Vilas, having given Chantal as thorough a scrutiny as she'd just endured from Rafe, finally released her. Her hand felt as though it had been branded by his tongue. The rest of her body was clamoring for more of the same.

"Do have a seat," Rafe said, ushering her to the table beside the window but not raising the blind. "Do you mind if Vilas and I have our breakfast while we talk?"

"No, go right ahead."

"Good, 'cause we both tend to be cranky when we're hungry."

"Do you need some light in here?" She reached for the blind. "It's kinda gloomy."

"No!" they said together.

Chantal dropped the blind cord as though it had scorched her. "Sorry, I just thought that—"

"It's very bright at this time of day," Vilas said, an edge to his voice. "The sun comes up on this side of the building."

"Fine." If they could see their hands in front of their faces, who was she to complain.

She turned at the sound of footsteps behind her. A small woman came into the room bearing two plates laden with what looked like steak. She wasn't wearing any shoes, either. Was that a company policy? Chantal wondered.

"Thanks, Rochelle," Rafe said as she placed the food in front of them.

"My pleasure." The woman turned toward Chantal. "Hi," she said. "I work the kitchen here. It's nice to meet you at last, Chantal." *At last?* "I just know we're going to be good friends."

Rochelle shot a look at Rafe and Vilas, almost as though she was saying she approved, and left the room. Chantal wanted to ask how they all knew who she was. Instead her attention was drawn to the food on their plates. It was indeed steak, huge quantities of it, and both guys set to work on it. Goodness, they enjoyed their steak rare. Vilas's plate ran with blood as he cut into it, making it seem as if the meat had argued with the frying pan and jumped ship.

"Sorry," Vilas said. "You must think us very rude. Can we offer you something?"

"Just coffee, thanks."

"You sure you wouldn't like some of this? It's really good."

"Er, I don't eat steak for breakfast."

Rafe winked at her, the gesture so suggestively sexy that it turned her insides to mush. "You don't know what you're missing."

Vilas disappeared into what was presumably the kitchen and returned with a steaming mug of coffee for her, along with a jug of thick cream.

"Thanks, but I don't take cream."

"You soon will," they said together.

Chantal had absolutely no idea what to make of this bizarre situation. She appeared to have been expected and was now sitting down to breakfast with two of the best-looking men she'd seen in her entire life. If they knew who she was, presumably they knew she'd come after the temporary position as bartender, but they appeared more interested in their breakfast than in asking her any pertinent questions about her employment history. Oh well, she had nothing else to do today anyway. It would be rude to interrupt them when they were both obviously starving. Hadn't they eaten dinner last night?

Presumably not, or they wouldn't be so ravenous this morning. They cleared their plates in record time.

"Okay, Chantal." Vilas turned toward her and offered her a full-wattage smile. It wreaked as much havoc on her feeble body as Rafe's wink had done just before. God, she was pathetic! "You're here about the job."

"Yes. I've got a lot of experience. I brought my résumé with me." She rummaged in her bag and produced the document, but neither man seemed interested in looking at it. Hell, don't say the position has already been filled. If so, why hadn't they said so and why was she still here?

"What brings you to this part of Florida?"

Rafe moved his chair back from the table as he spoke and crossed one bare foot over his opposite muscled thigh. Chantal couldn't take her eyes off his legs, and not just because, like Vilas, his jeans showcased a very impressive bulge. It was more the way he moved his limbs that fascinated her. Even when sitting, he seemed to be impossibly flexible. Images of him putting that flexibility to work on her body appeared determined to flood her mind. *Hell, don't go there!*

"I live in the north of the state, but I've come down here because my brother's gone missing."

"Missing how?" Vilas asked, frowning.

"If I knew that he wouldn't be missing. Sorry," she said when both men flexed their brows. "I guess it's a kind of sensitive subject." She took a deep breath, determined not to cry when she thought about the abrupt disappearance of her only living relative. "Max is a freelance troubleshooter for companies who are going through tough times. He goes in, tells them what he thinks they're doing wrong, and offers advice on how to put it right." *And judging by the state of this place, you could use his help.* "He went off on a job in Missouri six weeks ago and no one's seen or heard from him since then."

Vilas pulled both his legs up onto his chair and crossed them at the ankles so tidily that Chantal thought he must be double-jointed. It had to be excruciatingly uncomfortable, sitting that way on a hard ladder-back chair, and yet he appeared to be totally relaxed.

"I'm sorry," Rafe said. "He obviously means a lot to you."

She bit her lip. "He does."

"Perhaps he got another job."

"He would have told me. He's not answering his cell, or responding to e-mails." She shook her head. "It just doesn't make any sense. I've spoken to everyone he's ever worked with and no one's seen him." Chantal recalled whom she was speaking to and didn't elaborate. She'd only just met Rafe and Vilas and figured that they wouldn't be interested in her problems. "Anyway, to answer your question, I did one of my frequent Internet searches the other day, just to see if his name brought up anything new, and found this."

She rummaged in her bag again and produced the item she'd printed from the net. She barely had time to register that it had slipped from her fingers before Rafe and Vilas both reached for it, catching it way before it hit the floor. Their lightning-quick reflexes caused her to gasp. No one she knew was capable of reacting so quickly, but they didn't seem to think there was anything remarkable about what they'd just done.

"His name's mentioned in connection with a hotel renovation here," Rafe remarked. "Presumably you're hoping to track him down from there."

"Yes, I tried to get the people on the phone, but the guy I spoke to didn't seem to know much. I thought if I questioned the workers in person that might lead somewhere." She lifted her shoulders. "It's not much, but it's the only lead I have."

"I've not heard of a Max Lake hanging out in Impulse," Vilas said.

"I know it's a small town, but you can't possibly know everyone." The guys exchanged a glance that made Chantal feel she'd said something dumb. "Anyway, you need someone for a month, right?" she asked.

Chantal crossed her fingers as they took their sweet time answering her. She so needed a job with accommodation while she was in Impulse. She'd given up her office job back in Tallahassee because they wouldn't give her time off to come down here and look for Max, the cold-hearted bastards. She didn't have much by way of savings, still had rent and bills to pay at home, and so needed a job with accommodation.

"No we don't," Rafe said.

Shit! "Oh, but I thought—"

"We've got someone," Vilas added.

"We've got you," they said together.

"Well, it's great that you want to take me on," she said, now totally confused, "but don't you want to know a bit more about me first? I mean, I could—"

"We know everything we need to," Rafe said.

Chantal didn't see how they possibly could, but far be it from her to argue herself out of the job.

"When can you start?" Rafe asked.

"Right away."

"That's great. Your room's through here."

Chantal gulped. "I'll be living in this apartment with you two?"

"Yeah." Vilas flashed that sexy grin of his again, the one that made her cream her panties. "Is that a problem?"

"Er, no, I guess not. I just thought you wouldn't want a stranger cramping your style." Presumably they had women back here all the time. How could they not, two hunks like them? She was no voyeur. Anyway, she didn't like the idea of lying awake at night and hearing them fucking someone else.

"Not a chance."

"We open for breakfast at noon," Vilas told her. "You up for doing that shift."

"Breakfast at noon?" Chantal shook her head. "That's lunchtime where I come from."

Rafe grinned. "People around here tend to work on a different schedule."

"Obviously." She shrugged. "Sure, I'll start at lunch—I mean breakfast."

"Give me your keys, honey, and I'll bring your bags in for you," Vilas said.

This was all happening way too quickly, but it was what Chantal wanted, wasn't it? They hadn't talked about hours, pay, or anything like that, but she figured they probably wouldn't try to screw her out of a fair wage. If they wanted to screw her other ways, well, that was different. *Get real, babe, you're no oil painting, and these guys can take their pick.*

Ten minutes later she found herself alone in a roomy bedroom with an attached bath that was hers for the next month. She busied herself putting away the few clothes she'd brought with her, still feeling something was off about this setup. This room was way too sumptuous to be given over to staff usage, especially temporary staff, and the way the guys ran this business made the term *laid back* seem uptight and regimented.

What the hell? She wouldn't be here for long. Anyway, she had no time left to dwell upon the incongruities of her situation. It wouldn't do to be late for her first shift. Chantal changed into a tight-fitting pair of denim shorts and donned a pink vest that she knew suited her coloring. Eschewing sneakers in favor of flat espadrilles that were kind to her feet, Chantal rebraided her hair, took a deep breath, and was as ready as she'd ever be to report for duty.

Chapter Two

"She's here at last," Vilas said with a broad smile that Rafe knew encompassed both relief and anticipation. "I was beginning to think she didn't exist."

"Yeah, buddy, me, too. That's why I sent you such a loud pheromone. I know what you're like after a night out on the tiles. It usually takes an earthquake to wake you."

"Not when I knew our mate had put in an appearance." Vilas sighed. "Finally."

"She's the one," Rafe agreed. "No question."

"Those eyes, did you ever see such an unusual color?" Vilas closed his own eyes and rattled his tongue against the roof of his mouth in an appreciative purr. "Yellow with a hint of gold, wouldn't you say?"

"More russet and copper, like autumn leaves."

"It's all a matter of perception," Vilas said loftily. "Still, I'm sure we're on the same page when it comes to her reddish-brown hair. I lurve auburn hair and always imagined our mate would have a ton of it."

"Last week you said she was bound to be a brunette."

"Whatever." Vilas flapped a hand. "I can't wait to take her lovely hair out of that prim braid and run my paws through it."

"We've got a way to go before she'll let us do that," Rafe reminded him.

"There you go, spoiling my fantasies with details, just like always."

"I want her as much as you do, buddy, but we have work to do first."

"I could work on those curves of hers all day."

Rafe shot him a look. "Yeah, I hear you."

"Okay," Vilas said. "I know that look. You're trying to tell me not to get carried away. Our mate's turned up, we both know she's the one, but there's a problem to fix first, right?"

Rafe rolled his eyes. "When isn't there?"

"How come no one sensed she was here?"

"Because she's not a threat," Rafe said. "But whoever sent her is."

"Our enemies are using her to get at us?" Vilas frowned. "How?"

"Not sure yet." He picked up the résumé she'd left on the table. "She's worked at this place in Tallahassee for three years."

"And Tallahassee is close to where the lions hang out."

"Yep. I'm betting that they saw her and knew she was the one we were waiting for."

"Damned lions. Wish they couldn't pick up our pheromones."

"I'm also betting that piece about her brother was planted on the net."

"I'll check it out." Vilas picked up the printout Chantal had also left on the table. "We both know her brother can't be involved with hotel renovations in Impulse."

"Right." Rafe leapt from the floor and landed softly on one of the exposed ceiling beams on his fingers and toes, back arched. He draped himself across it, ten feet from the ground, always able to think better that way. It was almost as good as being in a tree.

"Whoever she spoke to about it wouldn't have been here in Impulse," Vilas said.

"Exactly. The person who set the trap by dropping that piece on the net was also set to take her call."

"But they couldn't have known that she'd go to the gas station and see our ad."

"No, not unless they're controlling her actions through mind manipulation."

Vilas sat bolt upright. "Shit, let's hope not."

"We'll have to check it out. Still, even if she didn't call at the gas station, it's a fair assumption that she'd have come here and asked about that hotel. This *is* the social center of Impulse, after all."

"True."

"My betting is that she'll get an e-mail from her 'brother' in a few days' time saying he's somewhere close by—"

"But not in Impulse where we can protect her."

Rafe nodded. "She'll go running wherever the e-mail points her to, having no reason to think anything's amiss."

"The lions know we, and the rest of the young males, will go after her, leaving Impulse open to a rogue attack."

"They'll be waiting for us when we go after Chantal," Rafe said. "But they'll also be waiting to invade Impulse as soon as we leave it unprotected."

"A double-fronted attack." Vilas nodded. "Sneaky bastards!"

"It's what I'd do."

"So what do we do now?" Vilas asked.

"First off I've sent a code-one pheromone out to everyone, telling them to be extra alert."

"Yeah, I got it."

"That's the easy part." Claws sprang from the ends of Rafe's fingers. He used them to scratch a particularly sensitive spot on his belly where a wound was healing, sighing with relief when he dealt with the pesky itch to his satisfaction.

"That cut still bothering you?" Vilas asked.

"It's healing, thanks. Anyway, the lions will act quickly," Rafe said, retracting his claws. "They have no choice. And if it isn't them, it'll be the werewolves or the bears using Chantal to get to us. All three gangs want to turf us out and use the place to their own advantage, but my money's on Boscombe and the lions. All of that means we have just a few days to introduce Chantal to the concept of us being panthers who prefer windows to doors, dislike bright light, and spend our nights roaming the national park because…well, because it's what we do—"

"That Impulse is a community of large cats and their human mates—"

"That she's the mate we've been waiting years to meet—"

"And she has the ability to restore our dwindling powers." Vilas growled. "It ain't gonna be easy."

"She'll be repulsed. You know how it was at first for some of the other humans who've mated with shifters."

"But she gets to share us both. How bad can that be?"

Rafe dangled an arm and leg negligently over the side of the beam. "You're thinking with your panther brain, buddy. Try getting the human one in gear."

"We both need to do that." Vilas seemed unnaturally serious. "Time's running out. Our enemies are getting desperate, and we're getting weaker by the day."

"Tell me something I don't know." Rafe squirmed, rubbing his belly along the beam and purring. "We have to attract her to our human side, make her fall in love with us, and, most importantly of all, get her to trust us."

"All in a couple of days." Vilas quirked a brow. "No pressure then."

"Get to work on the net, Vilas. We need to find out all we can about the ruse they used to get her here so we can try and second-guess them *and* thank them for it later."

Vilas's laugher came out as a low, rumbling growl. That shouldn't happen, which reminded Rafe of the trouble they were both having keeping their panther sides in check due to their loss of power. "You think?"

"Sure, they've done us a favor by sending our mate to us. We might never have found her otherwise."

"And I'd be stuck having sex with you for the rest of my days."

"Nope, you'd lose your ability to shift is all, and become a full-blown human instead. Then you could have sex with any woman you wanted."

"Tempting, but not worth losing my panther side for." Vilas twitched his nose, seeming surprised when his whiskers didn't move with it. "Besides, sex with you isn't all *that* bad."

Rafe rolled onto his back and touched his cock through his jeans. "I seem to remember you begging me to fuck you with this beauty last night."

"Only because you love it when I beg." Vilas blew a kiss toward Rafe's lofty perch. "I did it for you."

"Yeah, right."

"Stop touching yourself, Rafe. If you need to jerk off, I'll do it for you. You know how much you love having my lips clamped around your glans."

"I'll hold you to that later. Chantal turning up has made me as randy as a domestic cat."

Vilas flexed his jaw. "That bad, huh?"

They heard footsteps in the corridor leading from the bedrooms. Rafe landed on the floor on all fours, as light as a feather, and was sitting at the table beside Vilas when she walked in.

"Shit!" Vilas said pheromonetically. *"She's red hot. Look at those legs in those damned shorts. They go on for fucking ever. Hell, now I'm rock hard, too."*

"Her tits aren't too shabby, either. When I get my paws on them, she won't know what hit her."

"I absolutely can't wait to have sex with a woman."

"Not just any woman. Our woman. Our mate."

"Is something wrong?" Chantal asked.

Rafe realized they'd both been staring at her while they had a mental discussion about her attributes. Not the best way to go about putting her at her ease.

"Not a thing," he said, turning on the charm. No great hardship where his mate was concerned. "Vilas has a few things to finish up here, but I'll take you down to the bar and show you where everything is."

"Sounds good."

* * * *

As they made their way downstairs, Chantal noticed that Rafe now had shoes on, after a fashion. Cheap canvas jobs with the backs trodden down, like he couldn't stand to have his feet enclosed. There was a thin layer of dust over both sides of his black vest, making her wonder if he'd rubbed up against something in the storeroom while he waited for her to get settled. Ought she to tell him? No, it probably didn't matter if there was no one to see him. The bar had been empty half an hour ago and probably still was.

Rafe pushed the door open and Chantal was hit by a wall of noise. The place was packed with people, half of whom appeared to be eating steak as rare as that which Rafe and Vilas had just consumed. None of them had potatoes, bread, or vegetables with their protein, which seemed kinda strange. Then again, everything about this place struck Chantal as a bit weird, which made her have second thoughts about taking this job. If Max had come here and disappeared, would the same thing happen to her? If so, why didn't she feel more apprehensive about that very real possibility? Why wasn't she saying *thanks but no thanks* and getting the hell out of Dodge?

Chantal honestly didn't know why not. There wasn't much in Tallahassee for her any more. She'd moved there from the Midwest to be with the man of her dreams, but the cheating scumbag had put the kibosh on all that when he literally climbed into bed with his female boss. She still had a cheap rented apartment up there, a job she hated, and no friends because she'd had Jack and he'd convinced her they didn't need anyone except each other. Although, it seemed that he did, the two-timing shit. Chantal blew air through her lips, wondering how it was possible to reach the age of twenty-five and still be so naive. Anyway, she was here now, and however remote the chance of finding Max in Impulse might be, she wasn't ready to leave until she'd checked it out.

All conversation stopped as she and Rafe walked into the bar, and she was conscious of thirty or more pairs of eyes assessing her. None of the faces seemed hostile, more curious, and she felt slightly less conspicuous when several people smiled at her.

"Everyone, this is Chantal," Rafe said.

"We know," several voices said together.

"Hey, Chantal, welcome," said several more.

"Congratulations, Rafe."

A few men patted his shoulder as they walked past. One woman actually rubbed her cheek against his, which seemed an odd way to greet a person. She wondered what they were congratulating Rafe about. She wondered where they'd all appeared from so quickly as well, but had no time to dwell upon these oddities. Rafe sent the guy behind the bar back to the kitchen and showed Chantal where everything was. It was time to get to work.

"It seems pretty straightforward," she said. "Should I open the blinds?"

"We've got them," someone said, letting up the shutters on one side of the bar only, the side that didn't face the water or let in the overhead sun.

"Does everyone here drink milk?" she asked Rafe, glancing at the glasses beside the plates of meat.

"Not all." He nodded toward several other people eating what Chantal considered normal breakfast food—eggs, waffles, bacon, pancakes—and drinking coffee. "Milk's pretty popular at breakfast time, though."

"How come the parking lot's so empty?" she asked a little later when she returned from the storeroom, having taken a quick glance outside. The only car in the lot was hers.

"People in Impulse like to walk. It's a small town." He paused, following the line of her gaze, which was focused on his forearm. She hadn't noticed it before, but when he reached out to remove a plate from the bar, she saw a mishmash of thin white lines, similar to those on Vilas's torso, on the inside of his arm. "What happened?" she asked.

"A disagreement with an unruly customer."

"What did he hit you with? Those look more like deep scratches than knife wounds."

Someone called out to Rafe and he turned his back on her to answer the man. Chantal got the feeling that he'd deliberately dodged her question. She was starting to feel like Alice—curiouser and curiouser.

"You were telling me that Impulse is a small place," she said when Rafe returned his attention to her. "But it's not that small. Speaking of which…" She glanced at the customers perched on barstools, conversing amongst themselves but seemingly watching her with interest, too. "Does anyone know anything about a hotel called O'Malley's here in Impulse? Can you tell me where it is?"

Conversation died, and no one filled the heavy silence. Instead they all looked toward Rafe.

"I'll go through that with you after your shift."

"Oh, okay. I just thought someone here might know—"

"They won't."

Chantal didn't see how he could be so sure but was willing to let the matter drop, at least temporarily. Rafe was still behind the bar with her, not actually serving anyone. The rush had subsided and he left her to attend to any customers who still needed anything. He kept right on watching her like he couldn't quite believe what he was seeing. She felt his piercing gaze even when her back was toward him and wondered what it was about her that he found so objectionable. Why else would he keep staring at her? She didn't look bad enough to stand out, did she? Hell, it would be pretty difficult to achieve that ambition in a place like Impulse.

"I can manage if you have things to do," she said, tired of being in his orbit, especially since her body had woken up and taken more than a passing interest in the man. "There's no need to babysit me."

"I'm good right here."

"I won't run away with the day's takings."

Several people chuckled, which is when Chantal realized how alike a lot of them actually were. They had the same piercing blue eyes as Rafe and Vilas and they all growled rather than laughed. Yet they were different, too. Their facial features varied, but they were all blessed with above-average looks.

"Do you always get this many in for breakfast?" she asked.

"Nope." Rafe flashed a sexy smile that went straight to her pussy. "You've drawn quite a crowd, sweetheart."

"But no one knew I was starting work today. Anyway, why would they be interested in me?"

"You're a stranger."

"You don't get passersby in Impulse?"

"Sure we do, but not ones as special as you."

Chantal shook her head. For all the sense he was making, he might as well be talking in Swahili. She was tired of feeling as though she was the only person in the room not in on a secret. Before she could say as much to Rafe, a man with long, striped hair called out to him.

"We still on for tonight, Rafe?" The stripy man winked at Chantal. "Or do you now have other priorities?" He paused, as though listening to something and nodded. "Okay, Rafe, I get the picture."

How could he, Chantal wondered, when Rafe hadn't said a word?

"Can you reach me down a sack of that flour, Rafe?" Rochelle asked, poking her head around the kitchen door. She grinned at Chantal and pointed to a shelf a good ten feet above the bar.

"You doing okay so far, honey?" she asked.

"Yes, thanks," Chantal said. "I'll get the stepladder for you, Rafe."

Before she could do so, Rafe seemed to elevate himself from the floor with…well, with almost feline grace. She gasped when he reached the shelf, grabbed the sack, and landed again, all in one fluid movement.

"Oh shit," she thought she heard him mutter beneath his breath when he saw her gaping at him. "I shouldn't have done that."

Chapter Three

Rafe dragged himself away from Chantal, aware that he ought to leave her to it and go upstairs to see how Vilas was doing with his Internet search.

"Press the buzzer here if you need me," he said, pointing to a button beneath the bar. He would know if she had any problems before she even told him, but he didn't want to freak her out by telling her so. "It goes straight through to the apartment."

"I think I can manage," she said, glancing around the bar that now only had about half a dozen customers.

"Okay." He loitered, reluctant to let her out of his sight now that she'd finally come into their lives. No, he amended, now that she was here and had the ability to save their very existence. "I'll leave you to it."

"What time do we start serving lunch?" she asked.

"Oh, whenever people want it. They don't usually come in before five."

"I guess they wouldn't, seeing as how half the town has just eaten big enough breakfasts to keep them going for several days."

The locals' appetites appeared to amuse her, and she smiled at him as she spoke. The gesture lit up her entire face, enhancing her elfin features. It turned the copper in her eyes to a burnished gold and elevated her from averagely attractive to knock-out status. Her spontaneity went straight to Rafe's groin, causing him to half turn away from her so she wouldn't notice. He didn't want her to think he was a raving sex maniac, even if sex was all he'd been able to think about since she pitched up here this morning.

"You'd be surprised," he said. "People around here enjoy their food."

"That part I already got," she said, laughing.

"Don't discourage them, babe. It'd be bad for business."

"Okay if I take a break once I've cleared up here? I wouldn't mind taking a stroll around Impulse and…well, you know—"

"Give me a shout when you're ready. I'll give you the guided tour."

"No need. I'm sure you've got stuff to do."

"I insist."

When she didn't respond, Rafe decided not to push it. He took the stairs two at a time and kicked his shoes off the moment he got back to the apartment.

"How did she do?" Vilas asked, glancing up from his laptop.

"She did great. Half the town came to take a look at her, the rest are out on patrol." Rafe extended his claws, dug them into a thick rug, and stretched, arching his back until the joints popped. "Find out anything?" he asked when he'd loosened his limbs to his satisfaction and retracted his claws.

"She's definitely been set up," Vilas said with a rumbling growl. "She moved to Tallahassee about two years ago to be with some guy who lectured at the university."

"Where does she work?"

"She does office work for a retail outlet. She doesn't get paid well and doesn't have much by way of savings. Her mom and dad passed when she was still in high school. Her brother's several years older than her and took over as parent. I guess that's why they're so close."

Rafe scowled. "She still seeing the jerk at the university?"

"No. She caught him in bed with his much-older female boss."

"I take it you took a peek at her e-mail to learn a lot of this."

"Of course, but some of it's a matter of public record, like the deaths of her parents." Vilas shrugged. "As to the rest, I got creative, just like always."

"How recently did her relationship break up?"

"A couple of months ago. He swears he doesn't know how he ended up in bed with someone twenty years older than him, especially since he doesn't even like her and hadn't been drinking at the time. He's still at Chantal to take him back."

"So someone played tricks with his mind, making him do something that would get him caught so Chantal would be free for them to manipulate."

"No prizes for guessing who." Vilas hissed his disapproval. "That's where your buddy Boscombe and his pride of lions hang out."

"Tell me something I don't know."

"Boscombe's the worst of the lot. He'll never let up until he gets his grimy paws on Impulse and undoes all our good work here."

"Yep, which means our job just got harder." Rafe raked a claw through his hair as he thought it through. "We need to be absolutely honest with our mate. The problem is, if we tell her the guy she was supposedly in love with was set up, will she forgive and forget?"

"Let's keep that one back until we've won her trust." Vilas took his turn to stretch, growling when a hang claw caught on the rug. "What's she doing now?"

"Finishing up in the bar. Several of the colony are keeping an eye on her. She was getting suspicious about me hanging around so I figured I should give her some space."

"Yeah, don't crowd her."

"I couldn't stay near her like this. It wouldn't subside, and she'd have noticed sooner or later."

Rafe unzipped his jeans and his cock sprang free—rock solid, pulsating, and aching for action.

"My, my, we are a big boy today." Vilas rolled his eyes. "Get naked, buddy, and I'll sort it out for you."

Rafe was only wearing two items of clothing, as was Vilas. They were both down to their skin in a blink of an eye.

"Look who's talking," Rafe responded, nodding at Vilas's equally rigid penis—thick and angry and jutting almost all the way up his navel.

"We've waited fucking long enough for her. I figure we're allowed to get excited now she's finally here."

The two men fell into one another's arms, kissing passionately, their long panther tongues tickling their way seductively down one another's throats.

"You think she'll like being kissed like that?" Vilas asked when Rafe finally let him up for air.

"She'll like it just fine, once she gets used to it." Rafe placed a hand on top of Vilas's head. "Get down on your knees, buddy. You know what I need."

Vilas fell in front of Rafe, grabbing his swollen balls with one hand and his cock with the other. He massaged the former and wrapped his lips round the head of Rafe's prick, lapping delicately at the spot of creamy pre-cum seeping from it. Rafe closed his eyes and threw his head back as Vilas expertly sucked him down his throat, teasing him by tickling the underside of his cock with his rough tongue.

"Geez, that's so fucking good." Rafe pushed himself in and out of Vilas's mouth. "I'm gonna come for you, Vilas."

No sooner had the words left his mouth than he pulsated into Vilas's throat, an endless stream of semen shooting from his cock, draining his aching balls dry.

"Thanks," he said when he found enough breath to speak. He touched Vilas's rigid pole and smiled. "Got anywhere in mind for this thing?"

"Your ass is mine, buddy," Vilas replied, savagely pushing Rafe down on the rug. "Get on your hands and knees and be ready for a hard fucking."

"You think she'd like to watch us doing this?" Rafe asked, groaning as Vilas lubed up his fingers and rimmed Rafe's ass. "She might get turned on by it."

"She'll have to watch us sooner or later." Vilas replaced his fingers with the tip of his cock and plunged deep with one sharp thrust of his powerful hips. "Ahh shit, that feels *soooo* good."

"You've got that right. I'm getting hard again already."

"You want me to fuck your ass, buddy?" Rafe could hear laughter in Vilas's voice as he withdrew almost all the way, eliciting a groan of protest from Rafe. Vilas so loved to tease. "You want it, you gotta beg me for it."

"Just fuck me like you mean it and quit stalling. She could finish up downstairs any time now."

"And walk in on us." Vilas chuckled. "That'd be one way to cut to the chase."

"Probably not the preferred method."

"You imagining doing this to her ass?"

"Damned right I am."

"Think she'll let us?"

"She'll let us. You can sense how passionate she is just as well as I can. We'll just have to educate her and get her keen to experiment with the two of us."

"Get her to do as she's told and to beg for it." Vilas grinned. "I so want to hear her beg."

"Right." Rafe let out an elongated moan. "Shit, Vilas, give it to me harder. I'm gonna come for you again."

Vilas obliged, his heavy balls crashing against Rafe's buttocks as he drove himself as deep as he could get, hitting Rafe's prostate dead center with each thrust. He slapped Rafe's backside with the flat of his hand, while Rafe balanced on one arm, massaging his cock with the free hand.

"Let's come together," Vilas said, clearly straining to explode, his breathing labored as he drove himself closer to the brink.

"As long as you mean right now. Fuck it!"

Rafe howled as a shower of sperm shot from his penis. Vilas was right there with him. Rafe could feel him pulsating deep inside his ass as he came, and then came some more.

"Shit, she's left the place!"

Rafe jumped from the rug and pulled his two items of clothing back on. "I tuned out the pheromones while we were fucking—"

"Me, too." Vilas fell into his clothes, too. "Mikael was obviously trying to warn us." Vilas listened for a moment. "He says she's only just gone. We can catch her if we hurry."

"No. On second thoughts, let her explore on her own."

"But she'll find out O'Malley's doesn't exist."

"She would have done anyway. I asked her to give me a call when she was ready to do the town and said I'd go with her. She obviously wants to go alone. Let's give her some space."

"I suppose Impulse can be a bit overwhelming if you're new to it."

"Exactly, and I don't want her to think she's being stalked."

"I hate it when you're right all the time." Vilas got a cloth and cleaned all signs of their activities from the rug. "She won't decide to take off when she finds out O'Malley's is a blind, will she?"

"Whatever she decides, she'll come back here first. She isn't the type to cut and run." Rafe kissed Vilas deeply on the lips, squeezing his ass as he did so. "I love you so damned much."

"Yeah, me, too, and Chantal will make us complete. It was the thought of her watching us, or taking part, that added a new dimension to our fucking just then." Vilas touched Rafe's groin through the fabric of his jeans. "We absolutely can't risk losing her."

"We won't. Apart from anything else, her car's still in the lot."

* * * *

"Will you be all right on your own?" Rochelle asked, sounding rather anxious.

"Why wouldn't I be?" Chantal asked. "I'm only going out for a breath of air."

"Didn't I hear Rafe say he'd go with you?"

How the hell could she have? She'd been in the kitchen the entire time. "I'm good on my own. I'll catch you later."

Chantal grabbed her purse and headed for the door. She was starting to feel like she was in a prison without bars, the way these people were trying to dog her every step. Were they just being friendly, or was there something about the place they didn't want her to find?

"Stop being so fanciful," she chided herself.

She felt breathless again as soon as she walked outside. It was hot and humid, but it was more than just the heat getting to her. It felt as though there wasn't enough oxygen in the air to fill her lungs. One or two cars drove along at a leisurely pace, as though their drivers were having trouble building up a head of steam, too. There were quite a few pedestrians, and they all seemed to be moving at a rapid pace, so it must be her. She'd acclimatize soon enough, if she stayed, that is. She hadn't made up her mind about that yet.

She recognized one or two faces from the bar. They waved to her and she waved right back, but she didn't stop to chat. She needed to find the hotel that Max was supposed to be involved with and see where that led her. She'd picked up a tourist map at the gas station earlier and pulled it from her bag.

"It seems straightforward enough," she said aloud, appreciating the basic grid system. Even someone as brain dead as she was when it came to navigation could get her head round the simple layout. "All the hotels are on the Gulf side."

She refolded her map and headed in that direction, feeling light-headed from lack of oxygen. She only seemed capable of walking a few hundred yards at a time before needing to stop and rest.

"What is it about this place?" she muttered, leaning her hands on her knees, panting. Chantal was a regular runner and did five miles religiously each morning with rat-faced Jack back in Tallahassee before he did the dirty on her.

She leaned against a wall as she waited for her head to stop spinning. In spite of its lack of air, there was something soothing about Impulse. Under other circumstances she might consider settling here, but right now settling anywhere was out of the question. Until she found Max her life was on hold. He'd given up his adolescence to take care of her. No way would she bail on him now. There was something wrong, she absolutely knew it, and she wouldn't rest until she got to the bottom of it. She gulped back her anguish when she reminded herself that the only reason he wouldn't contact her would be if he was…was what?

"Stop being so fanciful," she said aloud when kidnappings, muggings, and murders sprang to mind. No one would kidnap him, and if he'd been in an accident she would have been informed. "All right, so why hasn't he been in touch?"

Impulse was certainly a tidy place, she thought as she continued to head for the stretch of hotels bordering a wide, sandy beach. She hadn't seen a single item of litter. All the gardens were pristine and…and what? Something was missing. It took her a moment to realize that although she'd seen a number of cats, there didn't seem to be a single domestic dog in Impulse. How strange was that?

She wended her way along the entire strip of hotels, which didn't take long. Impulse was at the extreme southern end of the bay, and seven miles of wide sandy beach stretched before her eyes. North of Impulse the resort hotels were tall and expansive. Impulse, by comparison, had very few. Those that were there seemed small and select.

Chantal frowned, wondering why Impulse wasn't cashing in on its fabulous location. None of the hotels they *did* have appeared to be undergoing renovation, and there was definitely no O'Malley's. She thought perhaps it was in a different location, but the receptionist in the hotel she stopped at to ask directions told her she'd never heard of it.

Deflated and out of time, Chantal made her way back to the Cat's Whiskers. She passed the Cat's Cradle Nursery as she cut through a different street. People in this town were obviously fond of cats. The gas station, she recalled, was called something to do with cats, and there was a restaurant along the hotel strip called The Lazy Lynx.

She let herself into the bar, totally wiped out by her short walk, wondering how she'd manage to drag herself up the stairs to the apartment. But the moment she closed the door on the outside world, her lungs cleared and she was once again full of energy. It was too surreal for words.

"What the hell," she muttered, bounding up the stairs, full of questions for the guys.

She pushed the door to the apartment open. Rafe and Vilas must have heard her on the stairs because they didn't seem surprised to see her.

"Hey," Rafe said. "Good walk?"

"Tiring."

"Yeah, it can be like that round here when you're not used to the heat."

"No, it's more than that." She shook her head. "I can't really describe it. I guess it's just something in the air, or not, in this case."

"A lot of people say that," Vilas said. "But you'll acclimatize."

"If I stay."

They shared a speaking look. "Why wouldn't you?" Rafe asked.

"Well, I couldn't find…" Her words trailed off and her blood pressure rose several points when her gaze fell upon two open laptops on the table, one of which was definitely hers. "What the hell do you think you're playing at?"

"Oh fuck!" Vilas said, following the direction of her gaze.

Chapter Four

"We need to talk." Rafe took Chantal's arm in a firm grasp and marched her to the nearest sofa. "Have a seat."

"Sorry, buddy," Vilas said pheromonetically. *"We got to fucking and I forgot about her machine still being out."*

"Don't worry about it. We need to set her straight about us, anyway. Might as well start now."

"It's too soon."

"She's spooked, so we have no choice. If we don't tell her something, she'll hightail it outta here."

"Will you two please stop staring at each other and tell me what the fuck you think you're doing with my laptop?"

"Don't cuss, sweetheart," Rafe said in a mildly reproving tone.

She rounded on him. "Just who the hell do you think you are, telling me what I can and can't say?"

Rafe sat beside her, but when he tried to take her hand, she snatched hers away. "I know how it must look," he said.

"You have no freaking idea how it looks, and I'm as mad as hell with you both." She placed her hands on her hips and glared at Rafe, then turned to treat Vilas, seated on her opposite side, the same way. "I'm a very private person. What right do you have to pry into my affairs?"

"It's not how it seems," Vilas said, spreading his hands and offering her a lingering smile.

"Oh really!"

"We didn't want to tell you this quite yet," Rafe added, "but I guess we have no choice."

"What you have is five minutes, and then I'm gone."

"Okay, we'll take your five minutes," Rafe said. "You'll probably think we're crazy, but if you hear us out I promise it'll make sense." *It had damned well better.* "You said earlier that you couldn't breathe well outside."

"What's that got to do with anything?"

"It's pivotal." Rafe inhaled deeply. "All of Florida used to have the positive ions in the atmosphere that still exist here in Impulse. Global warming and changes in the weather patterns over the centuries mean that only a very few places still have them."

"I still don't see—"

"Have you ever heard of shape-shifters?"

She laughed. "I go to the movies."

Vilas fixed her with a serious gaze. "Shifters aren't the product of Hollywood."

"You're right. I do think you're crazy." Rafe sensed that she was about to stand up and storm out. He sent out a mental command that stopped her in her tracks. A few weeks ago he could have done it without breaking a sweat. Today it caused him considerable strain, reminding him just how rapidly his powers were depleting. "This is some sort of sick joke."

"It's no joke, babe," Rafe said softly. "Everyone in Impulse is either a shifter or a shifter's human mate."

"And let me guess, you're all cats."

"Yep." It was Vilas who spoke. "Rafe and I are the alpha panthers in the colony."

"There are people you can see for these sorts of delusions, you know. Professionals who can get you the help you need."

"You're not making this easy for us," Rafe said.

"Okay, okay, have it your way." She threw her hands up. "You're big pussycats living in cloud cuckoo land, but I'm still out of here. Have a nice life." She tried to stand up, but this time Vilas threw out a mental order that seized up her limbs. "Damn, my legs won't work."

"Hear us out, then if you still want to leave, your legs *will* work."

She tossed them each a sarcastic smile. "Oh, so now you're taking credit for my cramps. That sucks."

"We have mental powers you can only dream about," Rafe said. "Unfortunately, they're on the decline."

"I suppose you expect me to ask you why."

"They're declining because Vilas and I need a human mate."

Chantal shook her head, a cross between a snort of laughter and a groan slipping past her lips. "I don't mean to toot your horn, but guys who look like you two do could have just about any woman they wanted." She paused. "Hang on, did you say *mate*? The two of you want just one woman between you?" She inhaled sharply. "This is getting weirder by the minute."

"The generations of shifters in our colony keep their powers by alternately mating with humans and their own species. If Vilas and I could choose a panther mate then life would be a damned sight less complicated for us than it is right now. Unfortunately, we have to find a human."

"But not just any human," Vilas said, taking up the story. "She has to be the right human. Once we mate with her, she will inherit some of our DNA and we'll regain our mental faculties."

"That's good to know," she said, rolling her eyes.

"We've waited more than ninety years for you," Rafe purred, running his fingers up and down her forearm. "What kept you?"

"Me!" She appeared dumbfounded. "Ninety years?"

"Three of your human years equate to one year for a shifter."

"You'll inherit that trait when you mate with us," Vilas said.

"In your dreams, buddy."

* * * *

"You've been in our dreams for years, darlin'," Rafe said in a strangely hypnotic voice that almost made Chantal think he was telling the truth. Almost.

"We're all different species of big cat here," Vilas explained. "Mikael, who you met in the bar earlier, is an alpha tiger, Rochelle is a lynx, and...well, I'm sure you get the picture."

"All that red meat," she said slowly.

"Yeah, now you're getting it. We're nocturnal, and because our powers are waning we need protein to kick-start our days."

"What about those who weren't eating meat?" she asked, unable to believe she was taking this seriously.

"Human mates."

Rafe smiled into her eyes as he spoke, and despite the fact that he was obviously stark raving mad, that smile still caused her nipples to tighten and her pussy to clench. Hell, perhaps she shouldn't think of it as a pussy anymore, given the circumstances. A screech of hysterical laughter rose up in her throat, but she managed to suppress it. Two insane people in the room were quite enough to be getting on with.

"Are you all right, darlin'?" Vilas asked, sounding as though he actually cared. "Can I get you anything?"

"Your reflexes," Chantal said slowly. "The way you got that sack of flour down in the bar..."

"You already feel so much a part of us that I forgot you weren't aware," Rafe said. "Sorry if I scared you."

"Not half as much as you are right now." Chantal made a massive effort to pull herself together. "All right, let's assume for a moment that I believe all this nonsense. Why do you say that I'm your er...mate?"

"Because you were sent here by our enemies," Vilas said. "That's why I was checking out your laptop. I had to be sure you were an innocent pawn."

"How did you get past my passwords?" She flapped a hand. "Oh, I get it, your mental powers."

"You've discovered that there's no O'Malley's hotel here, right?" She reluctantly nodded. "You've probably noticed as well that we can communicate with one another without actually talking." Another halfhearted nod. She *had* noticed all of the things they'd said but still wasn't taking them seriously. There had to be a more rational explanation. "Because there are so few places in this part of America where shifters can live *and* take advantage of the positive ions, Impulse is a prime target for others who want to take it over and oust us."

"Let's say that I still believe you." If she humored them, they'd let up on her and she could hightail it out of here. "Why not let other, er…shifters live with you?"

"We would," Vilas said, "if they were prepared to live in peace and not try to take over. Unfortunately, all those trying to oust us don't feel that way. Werewolves, bears, and lions are all out to get us."

"Lions?" Chantal felt faint. "But they're felines, too."

"Yeah, but they wanna rule our world." Vilas scowled. "I blame Disney for that. They actually believe all that hype about them being king of the jungle."

Chantal actually laughed. "Oh dear."

"Oh dear is right. The only good thing is that our enemies don't like each other any more than they like us. If they combined forces we'd never be able to hold on to Impulse. The lions have the edge because unfortunately, they can hear our pheromones."

"Your what?"

"Our silent communications. Theirs are on a different frequency to ours, too high for us to hear. It doesn't work the other way round though, and if they get close enough to Impulse, they can hear us and read our thoughts."

"Why can't they just stroll in and take over?"

"We put up a protective mental field round the town and know at once if anyone who comes in means us harm."

Chantal swiped her brow with the back of her hand. "I think I could use a drink."

Vilas leapt to his feet with…well, with feline grace. Without asking her what she wanted, he went to the kitchen and returned with a glass of white wine for her and bottles of beer for him and Rafe.

"Ah, so you do drink something other than milk?"

"Once we're up and running," Rafe said, winking at her.

Chantal took a healthy sip of wine. She sure as hell needed the alcoholic crutch. "I still don't get what this has to do with me."

"The lions have read our thoughts," Rafe explained.

"Bastard lions!" Vilas growled.

"They've tried all sorts of ways to get their paws into Impulse over recent months."

"Direct assault, stealth, coercing weaker colony members. So far we've been one step ahead of them."

"And so we think they've gotten inventive through necessity. They knew exactly what sort of mate we want, which would be you," Rafe said, focusing the full force of his piercing gaze on her profile. "They hang out near Tallahassee because there's still a small area outside the city, hotly contested, that has similar properties to Impulse on a smaller scale. We reckon they had a look round Tallahassee itself to see if anyone there fit the bill."

"They found you for us," Vilas said, "but you happened to be in a relationship at the time. They sorted that by getting into your guy's head and messing with it."

"Hang on, are you saying that a pack of lions—"

"A pride of lions," Rafe corrected. "And yes, they would find it easy to direct a human's actions through mind control. They're very good at it. They knew if your Jack cheated on you, you'd give him the elbow. With him out of the picture, all they had to do was find a way to get you down here."

"By using your brother."

Chantal's shoulders jerked upright. "They have Max?"

"Almost certainly."

"Here's the deal, Chantal," Rafe said, placing both of his hands on her shoulders and turning her to face him. "We'll help you find your brother, whether you agree to be our mate or not."

He eyes widened. "You can do that?"

"We can do pretty much anything we set our minds to," Vilas told her.

"All we ask in return is that you allow us to court you in the old-fashioned way," Rafe said, looking and sounding absolutely sincere. "We need you to fall in love with us so we can mate with you."

"And we also need you to be comfortable with us and happy to live in Impulse with the colony for the rest of your life," Vilas added, running a hand across her thigh, his touch so light and seductive that she almost felt like purring herself.

"I'll go to bed with you anyway if you help me find Max," she said without hesitation. In spite of the fact that they were a dime short of a dollar, just the feel of their hands stroking her body had her on sensual overload.

Rafe shook his head. "It's not that easy. If we mate with you, it's for life. You see, the moment we mark you with our semen, you become ours."

Chantal laughed. "What about all the women you've…er, *marked* before me."

"We haven't," Rafe said, a flash of pain marring his handsome features. "That's part of our problem. If we mark the wrong mate then it's almost worse than having no mate at all because our powers will diminish anyway."

"Hang on." She stared at each of them in turn. "Are you telling me that you've lived for ninety years and have never once had sex with a woman?"

They nodded in unison. "We're desperate, baby," Vilas said.

"I guess you must be." Chantal bit her lower lip as she thought about it. "So what do you do instead?"

"We fuck each other."

"Pardon?" Chantal gulped before sharing a glance between them. "Perhaps there's something in this crazy air of yours that's contagious, but did you just say that you fuck each other?"

"I know it's a lot to take in," Vilas said, continuing to stroke her thigh. "Just imagine how we feel."

"And we already warned you not to cuss. Do it again and I might have to spank that cute butt of yours." Rafe's fingers gently caressed the back of her neck. "Okay, you've gotten the gist of it. Now, if you still want to leave, we won't stop you."

That was absolutely what she ought to do. Max wasn't here, and she didn't seriously believe that he was being held mental captive by a pack...pride or whatever of lions, so she had no reason to stay. Even so, there *were* definite anomalies about this place, and Rafe and Vilas certainly had nonhuman qualities that weren't easily explained away. Besides, their hands innocently massaging her skin felt magical.

Chantal closed her eyes, willing the world to stop spinning for a while, just until she'd gotten this mess sorted. Or until Rafe's fingers made their way down to her aching tits. She really did need to get laid! She could only imagine how they must be feeling if...Hell, what was the matter with her? There was no *if* about it. Their story was bullshit. They wanted her here for some other reason, and she needed to find out what that reason was. To do that, she'd play along with them for just a little longer, *and* get a free massage.

"Everyone in the bar seemed to be...er, close," she said, her voice sounding more like a whimper when Rafe's fingers attacked the tangled muscles in her shoulders.

"We are," Vilas said. "It's us against the world."

"Do you like the idea of a close-knit family, babe?" Rafe asked.

Her eyes flew open. "How did you know that?"

His purring laugh, innocently suggestive, caused dampness to seep between her legs. How could she be so turned on by two such fruitcakes, albeit hunky ones? Dammit, she was a pushover—always had been.

"I'd like to impress you by saying I can sense the need for a loving family unit deep inside you," Rafe said. "Unfortunately, that wouldn't be true."

She rolled her eyes. "And you'd never lie to me."

"We haven't yet," Vilas assured her.

"You wear your need to be loved like a comfort blanket," Rafe said. "Your parents died when you were at an impressionable age and it was just you and your brother from then on in."

"That's why you'll do just about anything to find him."

Rafe nodded. "I'm betting that guys have taken advantage of your need to be loved ever since—"

"Especially that rat Jack," Vilas added, glowering.

"Jack strung you along, making dates and breaking them when he got a better offer," Rafe said. "He got you to move to Tallahassee so you could be at his beck and call. And the worse he treated you, the needier you became."

"Until you caught him with another woman," Vilas added.

They spoke like a tag team, finishing one another's thoughts without appearing to consult. The worrying thing was that they'd got it spot-on. She had been a doormat for Jack for far too long. She knew it and hated herself for being so lame. But any dream of happy ever after, however unrealistic, and a family unit all of her own to love and cherish, got to her every time.

"You *did* feel the family love in the bar," Rafe said.

"Yes, I suppose."

She was being economical with the truth and sensed that they both knew it. The feeling of community in that bar, the closeness, the caring, had been one of the first things to strike her. She'd put it down to small-town neighborliness, too concerned with learning her new job to dwell on the sense of oneness that had made her so comfortable. But thinking about it now, she'd felt safe and protected, warm all over. It was odd that it hadn't struck her more forcibly at the time.

Two pairs of piercing blue eyes regarded her closely as she recalled how pleasant it had felt to actually belong in a relationship where she wasn't the one to do all the giving. Regardless of whatever was *actually* going on here in Impulse, she somehow knew that if she was in trouble, any one of the people in that bar would have come to her aid, no questions asked.

"Yes," she said. "I miss what I had when Mom and Dad were alive. That's natural, isn't it?"

"Sure it is," Vilas said easily.

"It's a damned sight more natural than what we have going here," Rafe added. "Several different species of big cats all living together without scratching one another's eyes out."

"Just supposing that I believe you, how do you manage that?"

"We have a feline council, a bit like a city council, I guess," Vilas explained. "The alphas from each species are represented on it. We dispense our own justice and deal with any problems individuals might have."

"Don't you have an actual city council?" If they didn't, then perhaps she'd start to believe their crazy make-believe.

"Sure we do. Outwardly this is just another American town, which is just the way we want it. The city council is run by various felines' human mates."

"Of course it is!"

"We have fewer hotels because people can't stand the atmosphere here for too long. Some geologist made a documentary about our special atmosphere, decades ago now, telling people it was something to do with the fragmentation of the earth's crust."

"He was good looking and sincere," Vilas added, "so his findings kinda made it into folklore."

"With a little help from us." Rafe chuckled. "We don't like having visitors here for too long."

"But the colony does well from day trippers, coming down to see what all the fuss is about, buying souvenirs, stuff like that."

"Just what we need to keep our economy in the black," Rafe said. "We're not above commercializing what we have here if it keeps the werewolf from the door."

Chantal shook her head. "I did see a lot of souvenir shops, but still I can't accept what you're saying."

Rafe and Vilas looked at one another. Chantal got the impression that they were doing that pheromone communication thing again. Except that wasn't possible. It was probably just some form of mental telepathy, which wasn't the same thing at all, was it? Chantal wasn't sure she believed that either form of communication was possible. Rafe and Vilas probably just knew one another well enough to anticipate what the other was thinking, nothing more than that.

"We're going to have to show her," Rafe said, abandoning her neck massage and standing up.

Chapter Five

"She's still here," Rafe said. *"That's gotta mean something."*

"It means she wants to believe us."

"I sure as hell hope so. God, she's hot! So exactly what I always dreamed our mate would be like. Spirited, funny, feisty, and sexy as hell. I can't wait to bury my cock deep inside that tight pussy of hers."

"I hear you, buddy."

"Er, you don't need to go that far," Chantal said when Rafe pulled his vest over his head.

"Don't you like what you see?" Vilas asked in a teasing tone.

"I'm not looking," she said, placing a hand over her eyes, peeping between her splayed fingers anyway.

"I adore Rafe's broad chest," Vilas said, licking his lips as he massaged her thigh with the flat of his hand. "But I'm happy to share him with you."

"No need. He's all yours."

"Baby, you don't know what you're missing. He fucks like a god, trust me on this."

She pushed the hand he wasn't holding toward him, palm outward. "Way too much information."

Rafe laughed as he pulled his jeans off, at which point Chantal gave up all pretense at indifference. Perhaps that's because his cock was rigidly erect, twitching and straining as it jutted out from his pubic hair, reaching two-thirds of the way up his belly. He grasped it in one hand and massaged, his gaze glued to Chantal's face as he watched for her reaction.

"My goodness!" she said, blinking rapidly. "Do you have a license for that thing?"

"That's one of the benefits of being a shifter," Vilas explained. "I don't wanna sound immodest here, but we're pretty well hung."

"Er, yes, so I see."

Vilas leaned in close and whispered in her ear. "You fancy having both our cocks buried deep inside you, honey?"

Chantal moistened her lips. "What sort of question is that?"

"Go on, sweetheart, admit it. You're ever so slightly tempted, aren't you? Tell me the truth now. Your secret's safe with me."

"I've already told you that I'll hit the sack with you if you help me find Max."

Vilas slid his hand up the inside of her thigh. "And we've told you it doesn't work that way."

"Yes, but—"

"You ever had anal sex, sugar?"

"Have you ever had vaginal sex?"

A hiss of laughter from Rafe drew their attention back to him.

"What's he doing?" Chantal asked, shrinking away from him when his bones cracked and popped and sleek, tan fur covered his arms.

"He's shifting for you." Vilas abandoned her inner thigh and took her hand instead. "Don't feel afraid. He won't hurt you."

Strangely, after her initial shock, she didn't feel afraid. A situation that ought to have had her running for the hills made her feel not only curious but also strangely like she'd found the place where she belonged. She gripped Vilas's hand tightly for support and watched as Rafe slowly transmuted into a beautiful, sleek panther. She admired his creamy-white underbelly, the black tips on his tail and ears, and the way his eyes had turned bright yellow. He prowled toward her and rubbed his head down the side of her leg. His coat felt like silk, and without thinking about it, she reached out and scratched his ears. Rafe purred and rubbed his head against her a little harder, just as a domestic cat would in similar circumstances.

"I think he loves you," Vilas joked.

"He's beautiful."

Rafe purred even louder, rolled on his back, and exposed his belly. Laughing, Chantal reached down and scratched it for him.

"It's not fair," Vilas complained. "I should have been the one to shift for you, then I'd have gotten all that attention."

Chantal smiled. "What sort of panther is he?"

"He's one of the few native Floridian panthers left in existence, which is why he's the alpha."

"I thought you both were."

"We are, but there has to be a prima alpha, and that's Rafe because this is his territory. The rest of us are only here because his ancestors invited us in." Vilas lowered his voice, even though, presumably, Rafe could still hear him. "We have to pretend he's God's gift, otherwise he pouts."

"What are those lines on his belly?"

"War wounds. A damned bear tried to rip his guts out a few weeks back. That was a close one."

"A few weeks?" Chantal elevated her brows. "How come there's almost no scarring if the wound is that recent?"

"That's something else we need to explain to you."

"Why am I not surprised?" She flashed a distracted smile at Vilas. "And what sort of panther are you?"

"I'm all black, baby, and as smooth and erotic as your most sensual dream."

"He's all talk." Rafe had shifted back again while Chantal chatted with Vilas. He resumed his seat beside her but didn't bother to put his clothes back on. "You don't seem freaked out by what you just saw," he said.

"I'm not. That's what worries me."

"It proves that you're supposed to be one of us."

"There are fringe benefits," Vilas said, nodding toward Rafe's still-erect cock.

"So I see."

Rafe offered her a lazy smile. "You must have questions."

"Only about a million of them." She sucked her lower lip between her teeth. "What will happen to you if you lose your powers?"

"Aw, her only concern is for us," Vilas said. "I'm definitely in *lurve.*"

Rafe ignored Vilas's tomfoolery. "We'll become entirely human," he said.

"Would that be such a bad thing?"

"You live in the human world, baby," Rafe said. "You tell us."

"I suppose humans aren't always nice to each other, but it sounds like you lot aren't a whole lot better."

"Actually, we're the good guys, but we'll get to that in a minute. We'll become entirely human, but we won't lose our feral instincts."

"In other words, we'll be cats stuck in human bodies," Vilas said, shuddering. "A bit like a woman who feels she should have been born a man, I guess."

"At the moment, the reverse is happening. Because we're getting weaker, our feline instincts are stronger, like they're trying to remind us to find a mate."

"Which is why we need meat to get our days going, amongst other things."

"But you don't really understand what we do here in Impulse," Rafe said.

Chantal shook her head. "I don't understand much about anything."

"Did you see a large pink building when you went out today?" Vilas asked.

"On the corner of Main Street and First?" Both guys nodded. "Yeah, I saw it. What of it?"

"That's our clinic," Vilas explained. "It's what we do here."

"You asked about my injuries." Rafe pointed to the fine lines crisscrossing his stomach. Vilas pulled his shirt over his head and pointed out his as well. "That bear damned nearly ripped my guts out, but Vilas was able to get me back into Impulse just in time."

"The tigers are old-fashioned apothecaries," Vilas said. "They have a natural knack for it. A bunch of us go out on the prowl at night, into the national park, and collect certain plants that grow close to the shore there. The tigers boil them up, don't ask me how, and make this blend that heals wounds quickly, hardly leaving a trace."

"That's amazing."

"Yeah, it is, but they only work within Impulse."

"Inside your special atmosphere?"

"Right. And they don't stop at healing war wounds. They can also fix human diseases."

"Us shifters don't get regular illnesses like you humans," Vilas said. "And nor will you if you mate with us, babe." He winked at her. "That's a side benefit, built-in health benefits, along with getting fucked by us two, of course."

Rafe rolled his eyes. "Stick with the program, buddy."

"So you can only be killed by other animals?"

"We can't get diseases, but we can be run over by a bus, just like the next human."

"We, the tigers, that is, can also heal killer diseases in children that you humans haven't got a handle on yet," Vilas told her.

"You're kidding me." Chantal shared a wide-eyed look between them. "Like cancer and stuff?"

"And brain tumors." Rafe smiled at her. "Surreal, isn't it? That's partly the job of the feline council, deciding which cases to treat. Propositions are put forward, and we vote on the most-deserving cases."

"Then we send out mental commands that bring the family here. We treat the child and send them home again, wiping their memories so they don't know what happened."

"All they know when they get home is that their child is getting better, but not why."

"I don't understand." Chantal shook her head, like she was feeling dazed. Rafe figured that she probably was. "If you guys can do so much good, why not go public with it?"

"Because we'd be destroyed. Greedy humans would want to take over, just like the lions and bears are trying to. We'd be exposed as shifters, as freaks."

"Out shifter enemies want to profit from Impulse, and benefit from the slow ageing process. They can live elsewhere and still shift, but they age the same way as humans do, which is depleting their numbers. The good news from your perspective is that your ageing process will slow once you've mated with us." Rafe flashed a slow, sexy smile. "Not that I'm trying to put pressure on you or anything."

"The problem is," Vilas continued, "that we're not the only alphas in danger of losing our powers. The tigers and several other species are weakening for lack of suitable human mates as well."

"Now that we've found you, if we can persuade you to fall in love with us, at least we can get our powers back and hold the colony together until the others find their mates."

"You're making it very hard for me to say *no*."

"That isn't our intention." Rafe leaned toward her and softly brushed her lips with his. "That's why we hadn't intended to tell you any of this quite yet."

"The last thing we want is for you to feel coerced," Vilas added, rubbing his cheek against hers.

"I have another question," Chantal said. "You say the lions sent me here because they thought I'd make a suitable mate for you."

"Right," the two guys said together.

"But if they know your powers are weakening, why didn't they just leave you be, wait until you can no longer shift, and then move in?"

"Because, and we're guessing here," Rafe said, "they don't often get within range of our pheromones so they don't know how weak we actually are."

"And because they're running out of time themselves," Vilas added. "They're continually fighting with the bears and werewolves over that scrap of land outside Tallahassee *and* trying to invade us."

"Bottom line, all of our enemies are weakening and have lost quite a few of their number, but so have we. Finding mates for all our single alphas is now top priority and requires us to take a few risks."

"Okay, I get that." Chantal nibbled the end of her index finger, deep in thought. "So, I'm here. How does that help the lions?"

"That's where we're not entirely sure," Vilas admitted.

Chantal scowled. "That doesn't help much."

Vilas shrugged. "We said we'd never bullshit you, babe."

"But we can make an educated guess," Rafe said. "The lions know they won't get into Impulse undetected, and so they have to entice us out."

"We think they'll wait for you to get settled here, then send you some sort of message, an e-mail or something like that, purporting to be from Max. He'll say he's in trouble, you'll go rushing off to save him, and the lions know we'll come after you."

"They'll have us on neutral territory."

Chantal frowned. "Even if they do, and even if they manage to overcome you, there's still all the others here for them to worry about."

"We're a colony, babe," Rafe explained. "If we're in trouble then the other alphas, in fact all the male felines, will come to our aid. That's how we survive."

"So, you want me to stay here, fall in love with you, er...mate with you, as you so quaintly put it, and ignore any summonses from my brother." She shared a bemused look between them. "Did I leave anything out?"

Vilas waggled his brows at her. "You definitely got the mating bit right."

"Shut up, Vilas, can't you see we're upsetting our mate?" Rafe squeezed her hand. "We won't ignore the message from your brother. That's how we intend to find him."

"By letting the lions lead us to him," Vilas explained. "*Us*, not you."

* * * *

Chantal tried to absorb everything they'd told her, accepting now that it had to be true. Rafe's hand with its long, capable fingers wrapped round her palm sent spasms of warmth spiraling through her body. She squeezed her eyes closed when Vilas's palm returned to her thigh, expecting to wake up in her uncomfortable bed in Tallahassee and find she'd been having another of her erotic dreams. The ones that seemed to hit her whenever Jack had failed to satisfy her, something which happened most of the time. It didn't seem to occur to him that she faked her orgasms so as not to upset his masculine pride. It had never mattered to her if she didn't come. All she cared about was pleasing him.

Something told her that if she ever hooked up with these guys, not coming wouldn't be an option. Just the way they looked at her with such passionate intent made her inner thighs tingle with anticipation. She had to find a way to get them into bed and see if the reality lived up to her fantasies. She absolutely didn't believe that they'd leave her hanging unless she agreed to stay here permanently. After all, they were males, weren't they? Not that she'd ever be able to accommodate them both at once, as Vilas seemed to be suggesting. Lord have mercy, Rafe was probably too big for her cunt as it was. She'd never had anal sex but was pretty sure it would be even harder to fit either of them in that location. Even so, the idea of trying seemed to have lodged itself in her brain, and she couldn't shake it off.

If she had to, was she prepared to become part feline? She was unsure. Her life sucked the way it was right now. Her job was mind-numbingly boring, Jack, if she took him back, would still want their relationship to be conducted on his terms, and the happy ever after she still unrealistically dreamed about was never going to happen—at least not with him. Besides, there was Max to consider. She had absolutely no idea where he was, and now that she knew the guys were indeed shape-shifters, she had to believe that his disappearance was connected with them. The only way she could find him would be to hang around Impulse for a bit longer.

Besides, there was one other thing that she was curious about. More than curious, actually.

"What are you thinking, babe?" Rafe asked.

"Don't you know?"

"We try not to read minds unless the situation requires it," Vilas said. "It kinda takes the fun out of things."

"As well as being intrusive."

"And it drains our powers. We have to preserve our energy."

"That's a shame," she said with an artless smile.

The guys exchanged a look. "What's going on inside that lovely head of yours?" Vilas asked.

"Oh, nothing," she said, her tone implying just the opposite.

"Don't make me tune into you," Rafe warned.

"Like you already said, that's intrusive."

"Just tell us. I sense there's something you need to know."

"Well, since this is a day of firsts for me, I guess it won't hurt to tell you." She canted her head and smiled at each of them in turn, suddenly filled with a heady sense of control. These two gods were at her mercy, and well they knew it. "The thing is, I'm curious. I've never seen two men making out, you see."

Vilas's grin was broad and infectious. "She wants a show, buddy."

"Looks that way."

Without hesitation they both stood up. "Enjoy," Rafe said, kissing the top of her head.

Vilas shed his jeans, proving to Chantal that his cock, fully erect, was only fractionally shorter than Rafe's, but possibly a little thicker. She moistened her lips, which had become inexplicably dry, and settled back to watch the show. Rafe pulled Vilas against him so hard that their bodies collided with a loud thud. He squeezed his buddy's buttocks as he kissed him with depth and passion. Chantal suddenly felt like an outsider—a voyeur. These men clearly did love one another—there was no faking that type of passion. As a faker of some experience herself, she knew at least that much. She ought to leave them to celebrate that love in privacy.

Except part of her knew they wanted her to watch. Anyway, she couldn't have stood up if her life had depended upon it. She absolutely wanted to see this, and if they weren't happy about it, they wouldn't have started it, would they? She could just see their rigid cocks pressing against one another's bellies as they deepened their embrace. Sparks ignited inside her, and she felt desperate to join them. Somehow she resisted. She couldn't risk them losing control and *marking* her, or whatever it was they were supposed to do to her, unless or until she was absolutely sure it was what she wanted.

Rafe broke the kiss and reached for Vilas's cock.

"You're very big today," he said, massaging him with a heavy hand, squeezing his balls at the same time. "Wonder what turned you on."

"Can't imagine."

Chantal gasped when claws appeared at the tips of Vilas's fingers and he used them to rake Rafe's nipples.

"Christ, that feels good." Rafe squirmed and appeared to push himself closer to Vilas. "Give me some more of that."

"Like that, do you?"

"Yeah, I like it."

"Then ask me nicely. I need to hear you beg."

"Just focus on my nipples, fuck it, Vilas, and stop trying to pull rank. You know what it does for me."

"Told you his chest was worth exploring," Vilas said, flashing a glance Chantal's way.

Fascinated by what she was seeing, Chantal didn't realize that she'd pulled her top over her head until the guys broke their embrace and stared at her. She glanced down at her tits, encased in a red lacy bra.

"Perfect!" the guys said in unison.

"Did you make me do that?" she asked in an accusatory tone.

"Do what?" Vilas asked, a little too innocently.

"You know what. I don't usually strip in front of strangers."

"We're not strangers, babe," Rafe said, turning toward her and taking a step closer so that his rigid cock was level with her face. "We're your mates, if you'll have us."

"Stop delaying and get over here and fuck me," Vilas demanded, throwing a tube of lube Rafe's way.

"Duty calls," Rafe said, blowing a kiss to Chantal and catching the tube one-handed. "Lean over Chantal," he said to Vilas. "Put your hands on the back of the settee and spread your legs."

Chantal now had Vilas's rigid cock straining just above her face. The urge to stick out her tongue and taste him was irresistible so she did just that. Vilas groaned.

"Baby, you are absolutely the answer to my prayers." Vilas shifted a little as Rafe lubed a finger and inserted it in his anus. "You wanna join us?"

"I thought I couldn't."

"You could take your bra off and let me come over your lovely tits."

With a reckless laugh, Chantal reached behind her, unfastened her bra, and cast it aside. She was aware of both men barely breathing, watching her intently. Just to tease them, she covered her naked breasts with her hands, allowing just the dark nipples to peek through her fingers.

"Geez, she'll be the death of me yet," Vilas complained.

"Don't move," Rafe ordered Vilas as he stepped around him, fell to his feet in front of Chantal, and pulled her hands away from her breasts. "Let me introduce myself," he said.

With Vilas's cock dangling above her face, Rafe applied his lips to one of her nipples. It was rock hard and super sensitive. Rafe sank his teeth into it and she screamed as pleasure spangled through her in unstoppable waves.

"I knew she'd be responsive," Vilas said, satisfaction in his tone.

Chantal's panties were sodden, as were her shorts. Both items of clothing were completely useless. She wanted to remove them and feel as free and uninhibited as Rafe and Vilas obviously did.

"Take them off," Rafe said, removing his lips from her tit, second-guessing her, reading her thoughts, or whatever it was that he did to be so in tune with her. "We want to see all of you."

She wiggled out of her clothing without standing up and then spread her legs, giving both men a good look at the pink lips to her pussy.

"Like what you see?" she asked in a provocative tone she'd never used with anyone before.

"Absolutely! Just the thought of sinking my cock in that gorgeous pussy is driving me demented." Rafe tilted his head. "Unbraid your hair for me, darlin'."

Chantal did as he asked, combing her fingers through her hair when it fell loose. It tumbled in a tangle of waves halfway down her back. Both men smiled and took it in turns to dip their heads and kiss her. And what kisses they were. Unworldly, or not like any world she'd ever known, was the only way she could describe them. Rafe's lips seemed to devour her own like he never wanted to let them go. Vilas's hand tweaked one of her nipples, setting Chantal on fire. Rafe's exceptionally long tongue plundered her mouth and Chantal lost herself in sensory heaven. She never wanted the moment to end, and when Rafe eventually broke the kiss a small moan of protest slipped past her lips.

"Let Vilas come over your tits while I fuck his ass," Rafe said, his words a softly couched command that Chantal didn't even think about disobeying. Alpha males, she was fast discovering, had a lot going for them.

"Can I suck him?"

"Can you suck me? Are you kidding me?" Vilas grinned like an idiot. "Be my guest, honey."

Rafe returned his attention to Vilas's ass, slapping it hard with the flat of his hand. The harder he hit, the more subservient Vilas became and the more he appeared to enjoy it.

"Would you like us to slap you when the time comes, sugar?" Rafe asked.

"I'm…er, I'm not sure. I've never been spanked before."

Vilas winked at her. "You don't know what you're missing."

"I think we're getting ahead of ourselves a little. I haven't agreed to mate with you yet."

"Just think of the fun you have in store then."

"Who gave you permission to speak?" Rafe asked, hitting Vilas's ass even harder.

"Sorry, buddy."

"So I should fucking well think. Get down on your knees so I can screw you even harder for being so disobedient."

As soon as Vilas adjusted his position, Rafe thrust brutally into him, burying himself to the hilt and sighing with pleasure when he got where he needed to be. Far from hurting him, Vilas appeared to love it since his cock jerked to even greater heights in front of Chantal's face. She leaned forward and sucked its head between her lips, running her tongue across his glans, unable to resist teasing him because she had him at her complete mercy.

"Oh God, this won't last two seconds with her doing that." Vilas moaned. "She's so fucking good at it."

Chantal sucked more of him into her mouth, tantalizing the underside of his cock by tickling it with her tongue.

"You are not to come until I say you can," Rafe said, pumping hard into Vilas and slapping his ass with both his hand and his laden balls.

Chantal reached for Vilas's balls and put gentle pressure on them.

"I can't fucking hold it," Vilas screamed. "She's killing me. You both are. Fuck me, Rafe, and you, darling, I'm gonna come for you both."

He shot his load deep in the back of Chantal's throat, panting and moaning as Rafe continued to pummel his ass. Chantal swallowed repeatedly, struggling to keep up with his seemingly endless flow of cum. Vilas's entire body trembled as he found release, but Rafe didn't let up on him, not for a moment, and kept hammering into him. Only when Vilas finally stopped screaming and Chantal released his now-flaccid penis from her mouth did Rafe let himself go.

"Get round here, Chantal," he said, "and grab my balls. I'm gonna come."

She squatted beneath him and laved his balls with her tongue. Rafe groaned. With one hand on the top of Chantal's head, his body tensed, his balls pulled tight, and he ejaculated inside Vilas's ass, a stream of filthy language spilling from his lips as he did so. He withdrew when he was finally done, released his hold on Chantal's head, and smiled at her.

"Okay, babe," he said. "Now it's your turn."

Chapter Six

Chantal seemed bemused. "But you said—"

"Come with us." Rafe held out a hand. "We've got something you need to see."

"Er, shouldn't I be getting back to work?"

"It'll still be quiet down there," Vilas said. "Anyway, we've got it covered."

All three of them were still naked. Rafe wondered if it would bother Chantal to be without clothes that way when they were no longer fucking. He and Vilas were usually naked when they were in the apartment. They were more comfortable that way. Chantal didn't seem to be the slightest bit inhibited by her circumstances. Why would she be? She had a body to die for—slim, shapely, and simply made for loving. Rafe and Vilas shared a glance that said if she didn't agree to mate with them real soon then they'd go out of their minds.

They'd managed all these years without a woman. Now that the right one had come along, their legendary patience was fast running out and they couldn't wait to make up for lost time. The restoration of their mental abilities had been their main objective these past several months. Nothing had been more important. Rafe was astounded to find that that prospect barely registered on his radar anymore.

Instead he was obsessed with the need to impress Chantal, to make her fall in love with them and agree to become their mate. He'd known deep within his soul—his human soul *and* its panther counterpart—the moment he sensed her presence that she was right for him and Vilas. She was the only woman in the universe who possessed what it took to make them both happy *and* ensure the future of the Impulse panther population.

Vilas opened the door to the room that he and Rafe shared and both men stood back, letting Chantal enter first.

"What do you see?" Rafe asked.

He and Vilas watched her as her gaze encompassed the entire room. It was large with a window that opened directly onto the roof—convenient for nocturnal wanderings—but most of the space was occupied by a massive bed.

"Is this the room you two share?" she asked.

"Yes."

Rafe ran a hand lightly across the back of her neck. She was still rigid with tension, which was hardly surprising given all she'd just seen and learned. Rafe was impressed by her ability to take everything in without falling apart, but then again he'd expect nothing less from the resourceful female destined to become their mate.

"Why are you showing me this room?"

"Because you need to understand just how long we've been waiting for you," Vilas said, earthy sincerity in his tone. "We sleep in this bed every single night—"

"Well, day really," Rafe amended. "We're nocturnal and tend to sleep when it gets light."

"All those closed shades," she said, nodding slowly. "You're sensitive to daylight."

"We are when we're as weak as we are right now."

Chantal narrowed her eyes at each of them in turn. "I hope you're not trying to guilt me into mating with you?"

"Absolutely not." Rafe arranged his features into an expression of resolute determination. "This is a lifetime commitment, babe, and you need to be absolutely sure before you sign up. We don't have divorce here. If you're in, you're in for good. That being the case, it's a big step—"

"You don't say."

"We won't accept you as our mate, even if you beg us to mark you, unless we know for sure it's what you want."

"And we will know," Vilas warned her.

She rolled her eyes. "Of course you will. I need to be careful what thoughts I have when I'm around you guys. A girl needs her privacy."

"We'll teach you how to block us," Rafe said. "We don't mean to be nosy, but sometimes we just can't seem to help ourselves."

"Okay." Chantal nodded. "That seems only fair. So why are you showing me this room if you don't want to ravish me on that very comfortable-looking bed."

Vilas groaned. "Trust me, honey, we do."

"But we're not going to." Rafe placed his hands on her shoulders and turned her until she was looking only at the bed. "Vilas and I sleep here together, but we have never fucked one another in this bed."

Chantal blinked. "Why ever not?"

"Because we want to christen it with our mate," Vilas said. "I sleep on that side, and Rafe crashes out on the left. There's acres of space between us, no touching allowed. That lovely gap in the middle with all those squidgy pillows is reserved for you, our mate."

"Or someone else."

"No, love," Rafe said with determination. "You're the one, even if you haven't accepted that fact yet."

"You haven't exactly given me much time."

"True." Vilas nodded. "We're prepared to wait."

"Presumably the rugs in the living room are there for you to have your fun on," she said.

"Absolutely." Rafe laced his fingers with hers and led her back that way. "And that's where you're going to play with us now, if you're willing."

She offered each of them a radiant smile. "Like you said just now, it's my turn."

Vilas chuckled. "The lady's hot."

She fanned her face with her free hand, making them both chuckle. "After watching you two in action, can you blame me?"

"If you could remain immune while watching me fucking Vilas then you wouldn't be the mate for us," Rafe told her. "In case you hadn't noticed, we like sex."

"Lots and lots of sex," Vilas added, presumably to ensure that she was left in no doubt.

"What are you planning to do with me?" she asked as they reentered the living room.

"That's for us to know and you to find out," Rafe said. "When it comes to fucking, I'm in charge and whatever I say goes. If you don't do as you're told straightaway, you get punished."

"I see." Chantal's eyes sparkled and she bit her lower lip, her expression pensive. "But what if I don't like what you do to me?"

"You will, but if for some weird reason you don't, just ask us to stop and we will."

"All right. That seems fair."

"You must behave submissively in our presence at all times, and speak only when spoken to."

"What should I call you?"

"You refer to us both as 'sir' or 'master'."

She stood in front of Rafe, lowered her eyes, and rubbed her thighs together. Vilas noticed and tapped her butt.

"Leave that to us. We'll make you come and come, and then come some more. You'll be screaming at us to give you it, baby."

"Lay flat out on that furry rug, Chantal," Rafe said, his voice resonating with authority.

She did as he asked, moving so fast that she almost tripped over her own feet. Vilas and Rafe towered over her, feasting their eyes on the sight of their naked mate, lying there totally uninhibited, waiting for instructions. Her eyes were hazy, a sultry smile playing about her pouting lips, and her nipples very obviously rock hard. Rafe was willing to bet that her pussy was damp as well, and that her clit was throbbing in time with her raging hormones.

They hadn't had full intercourse with a woman, but they'd played games with enough of them to know how to give satisfaction without penetration. That had always been enough for Rafe. He knew what responsibility he bore for the future of his species and wasn't prepared to mess with that. Penetration hadn't seemed that important when balanced against such weighty responsibilities. He could get his female playmates to suck him off and, if he needed to fuck, Vilas was always willing to offer up his ass.

Suddenly, looking down at his sinfully tempting mate to be, he couldn't get the thought of penetration out of his head. He could mark her right now—he was sure she wouldn't object—and then they'd be mated for life. It wasn't the way he'd planned to do things, obviously, but he'd make sure she never regretted the lapse in his normally rigid control.

"Don't even go there," Vilas pheromoned. *"She has to make up her own mind."*

Rafe sighed. *"I know that, but she's fucking killing me, the witch."*

"Me, too, buddy, me, too, but we'd never forgive ourselves if we forced her."

"No, no, you're right, but I can't stop thinking about sinking my cock into that tight pussy."

* * * *

Chantal wiggled into a more comfortable position on the thick rug, willing the guys to get down to business. Not being able to speak and having to do whatever they told her was a massive turn-on. No one had ever done anything like that with her before. Not that she'd had that many lovers, but those that she had allowed into her bed, she was starting to realize, had been more interested in their own needs than in hers. She'd been so desperate to be loved that it hadn't occurred to her to mind.

Things were different now. She knew what she wanted. The sight of Rafe and Vilas fucking one another had unlocked something inside her, and she was no longer prepared to settle for second best. Not much chance of that. Just the thought of two such gorgeous hunks as Rafe and Vilas giving her their undivided attention made her shiver with desire.

"Are you cold, Chantal?" Rafe asked.

She shook her head, unsure if she was permitted to speak.

"You can answer me," he said. "If I ask you a question, you must always answer it."

"No, sir, I'm not cold."

"Then why did you shiver?" Vilas asked.

"I'm aroused. I like the thought of you two playing with me."

"Do you now?" Rafe crouched beside her, as lithe and graceful as…well, as a panther. "And what would you like us to do to you, sugar?"

"Make me come." She shared an imploring glance between the two of them. "Please make me come, masters."

"You sound kinda desperate," Vilas remarked in a lazy drawl. Crouched on her opposite side, he blew softly on one of her nipples. Taken by surprise, Chantal screamed as sensation coursed through her, causing both men to laugh.

"She is close to the edge," Rafe said. "Raise your arms above your head, Chantal, and we'll see what we can do to ease your ache."

As soon as she did so, Vilas tied them to the leg of a sturdy sofa while Rafe fixed a blindfold over her eyes. Chantal gulped, wiggling her ass in an effort to find some relief from the desperate need that blotted everything else from her conscious thoughts. She'd never been tied up before, nor had she been blindfolded. Far from feeling apprehensive, being at their complete mercy was such a turn-on that she was ready to explode.

"Keep still," Rafe said. "We've removed your senses of touch and sight, which ought to highlight your reactions when we put our hands, or whatever else we decide to use, on you. Are you comfortable with that?"

"No."

"What's wrong?" they asked together.

Chantal didn't care how needy she sounded. They had to know the truth. If she didn't tell them, they'd probably just read her mind anyway.

"I'm in agony," she said. "I so need to come that if you don't do something about it pretty damned quick, then I'll have to take care of it myself."

"Without your hands," Vilas taunted.

"I only need to rub by thighs together. The way I feel right now, that ought to take care of it."

"Okay, baby." Rafe's smooth tone immediately silenced her. "One of the other fringe benefits of mixing with us is that panthers have very long, very flexible tongues."

"Would you like us to lick you all over?" Vilas asked.

Chantal nodded vigorously. "Yes."

"Ask us nicely then."

"Please, masters, please lick me all over."

"Spread your legs for us, honey," Vilas said.

Chantal did so, moaning softly as anticipation swelled deep inside her. Someone picked up one of her feet and sucked each of her toes into his mouth. Chantal had no idea that toe sucking could be so sensory. It sent waves of pleasure straight to her sodden pussy. She'd barely gotten used to that sensation before someone else kissed her, hard and deep, a tongue so long it seemed unreal working smoothly all the way down her throat. Chantal decided to get some of her own back. She clamped her lips round that tongue and sucked on it as hard as she could. When its owner groaned, she thought she recognized Rafe's voice.

"The little witch tried to turn the tables on me."

It *was* Rafe. Chantal kept her smile in check. He might think he was in control here, but he'd failed to take into account the power of her femininity. They'd released her demons, made her aware of what she *could* be. It was truly liberating. Right now, she felt she could conquer the world singlehanded, so these two panther-people should be a breeze by comparison.

Something scratched at one of her nipples, touching it so softly that at first she thought she'd imagined the feeling. But no, sensation streaked through her and she instinctively lifted her torso, desperate for more. Two masculine chuckles rang out and the pressure increased. It was the most exquisite agony. She expected at any moment for a hand to massage her entire breast and pinch at the nipple.

It didn't happen.

Instead the tantalizing scratching got a little harder, almost making her delirious.

It was impossible to keep still when her body was being attacked from both ends simultaneously. She squirmed, spreading her legs even wider, willing one of them to touch her pussy. That's all it would take. A couple of strokes across her clit and she'd be in heaven. Why were they taking so damned long about it? She wanted to scream with frustration. Afraid they would see that as rebellion and slow down even more, she forced herself to keep quiet.

"Keep still, Chantal," Rafe said, tapping the side of her thigh. "No one gave you permission to move."

It had to be Vilas sucking her toes, except he'd stopped doing that and was now licking his way slowly—so slowly that she thought she might well die of anticipation—up her calf. Every so often he took tiny nips at her skin that only increased her inexorable need. God, but they knew how to torment her! If they didn't give her an orgasm soon then she'd probably agree here and now to be their mate.

Both of her nipples were now being scratched and Vilas's tongue had reached her inner thigh. He would come up against her coursing juices soon, but she simply didn't care. She'd swallowed everything they produced just now, so it was payback time. Sure enough, Vilas emitted a sound that could have been a growl or a purr when his tongue reached the liquid that was the essence of her. He lapped at it, delicately at first, and then in double-time. She could tell from the noises he made, and from the sensual sweeping of his tongue, that he was savoring every drop.

Chantal's entire body shook with anticipation. The hell with remaining still! It was completely beyond her capabilities to do so when she was so aroused. She'd never been big on passivity. Their creative energy and the physical alchemy that appeared to exist between the three of them drove her increasingly wild. She'd never felt this abandoned about sex before, but then she'd never experienced it with more than one guy in the past. Perhaps that explained her desperation. She neither knew nor cared. Right now she was living for the moment.

She lifted her legs, hoping to find Vilas's shoulders. If she hiked her feet over them, surely he wouldn't be able to resist her pussy. The moment she moved they both stopped what they were doing to her. Chantal whimpered.

"Who said you could move?" Rafe demanded.

"Enough!" she cried. "You said I could call a halt any time I felt like it, so that's what I'm doing."

"You don't like our methods?" Rafe asked, sounding like he knew the answer to his own question, arrogant panther-person that he was.

"I need to come," she wailed. "You promised me. 'You'll come and come, and then come some more,' were your exact words, Vilas."

"Yeah, I did say that, didn't I?" She could hear the taunting smile in his voice. "I guess we'd better overlook her rebellion just this once, Rafe, given the circumstances."

"Looks that way," Rafe agreed. "We'll get her trained up soon enough. We've got the rest of our lives to do it in."

"I didn't agree to—"

"Shush!"

Vilas returned his tongue to her thighs but this time didn't linger. It swirled its way toward her clit, tantalizingly close, as two fingers slid into her vagina. Chantal pushed against them, lifting her hips to force them deeper. Vilas's tongue flicked across her clit and ignited scorching sparks of desire deep within her core.

"Yes!" she cried. "That's it, Vilas. It feels so damned good."

"No talking!" Rafe tapped the side of her thigh again. Then his mouth descended on one of her tits and bit playfully at the nipple. It was all it took to send her over the edge. She screamed the roof down when her climax hit like a minitornado, taking her completely by surprise. It was harder, deeper, and more intense than anything she'd ever known before. Her entire body convulsed as she rode Vilas's fingers until he'd milked every last ounce of sensation from her body.

"Oh God!" She continued to tremble long after her climax subsided. "What the hell did you do to me?"

"Gave you what you asked for," Rafe said, "even though you didn't deserve it because you didn't obey orders."

"Sorry, master," she said meekly.

His lips covered hers. "Ready for round two?" he asked when he eventually stopped fucking her mouth with his magical tongue.

"There's more?"

"Baby," Vilas's voice said. "We've barely got started."

The blindfold was removed and then her hands were released. "What did you touch my tits with?" she asked, blinking to readjust to the light.

Rafe showed her a fierce claw bulging from the tip of his index fingers. "Only this."

"But, that ought to have scratched me to pieces. I thought you were using a feather, or something."

"I knew you wouldn't let me use this if you saw it. That's why I blindfolded you." He smiled at her, looking thoroughly pleased with himself.

"It's called sensation play," Vilas explained.

"I know how good it feels to have your nipples clawed. I love it when Vilas does it to me."

"I don't have claws to offer, but do you think you'd like it if I sucked your nipples?" she asked Rafe.

"Geez!" Vilas said, running a hand through his hair.

Rafe canted his hand and flashed a sexy smile that brought her pussy zinging back to life. "I reckon I could put up with it."

Rafe extended one hand and pulled her to her feet like she weighed nothing at all. He was fully erect again, she noticed, as was Vilas. He sat on the settee she'd been tethered to and told her to straddle his legs.

"But that means—"

"Don't question me, babe," Rafe said, tapping her butt in admonishment. "Just do as I ask. I won't penetrate you."

Chantal got herself into position and enjoyed the feel of Rafe's stiff rod pushing against her clit. She also got an up-close and personal view of his broad, muscular chest. Never one to look a gift panther in the face, she dropped her gaze and then her lips to his left nipple. She took a leaf out of his book and nipped at it. If she had claws she'd have used them, too, damn it. He groaned as she employed her teeth, lifting his hips so that his cock rubbed against her sensitized pussy. Encouraged, Chantal leaned forward and raised her ass in the air, the better to feel his erection where she wanted to feel it the most.

Well, almost the most.

She moved with Rafe and bit a little harder at his nipple. As she did so she was conscious of something cool hitting her ass. Shocked, she stopped moving.

"Shush, it's okay," Vilas said from behind her. "Don't mind me. Carry on with what you were doing."

The feel of Rafe's prick pressing even harder against her sodden pussy reclaimed her attention. Fire lanced through her veins and she was dangerously close to another orgasm. She tried to think about something else, determined this time to hold it back for as long as she could. Then she felt something invade her anus and tensed.

"Relax for me, babe," Vilas purred. "Let me investigate."

Presumably he'd inserted a finger in her backside. No big deal. People did that sort of thing all the time. It was high time she found out for herself what all the fuss was about. Vilas caressed her ass with smooth sweeps of one large hand until she relaxed.

"That's it, honey," he said. "You've got two of my fingers right up your ass now. How does it feel?"

"It burns a little, but it's okay."

Rafe chuckled. "Only okay, buddy. You're losing your touch."

"Just wait until you have one of our cocks up your pussy and the other in your ass. Imagine how that will feel."

"It's not possible. You're too big for me."

"We'll prepare you so that we won't be, never fear," Rafe said, increasing the pressure on her clit until she moaned. "That's it, babe, thrash your head round for me and make all that hair tumble all over the place."

Chantal forgot all about playing with Rafe's nipples and simply gave herself over to pleasure. Tingling exhilaration spiraled through her, fragmenting her senses when Rafe gave one massive upward thrust that ignited the orgasm she'd been trying to delay. God alone knew what Vilas was doing to her ass, but whatever it was, the sensation was growing on her. She cried out as pleasure beckoned, release so tantalizingly close and yet seemingly just out of her reach.

"You're so goddamned beautiful, Chantal. Come for us, baby," Vilas coaxed.

"It's not enough," she wailed. "I need you to fuck me."

"Can't be done, angel," Rafe said, his voice clouded with regret. "You know that."

"Yes, but...argh, that's it. I'm coming for you now."

"Feel my cock on your pussy," Rafe urged, slamming it against her clit. "Feel what it does to you."

"You wish it was us inside you, don't you, sugar," Vilas purred from behind her. "You'd give anything right now to have us both."

Chantal didn't have enough spare breath to answer him. Anyway, what would be the point? They wouldn't penetrate her unless she agreed to be their mate, and it was way too soon to consider their crazy proposal. Even so, the temptation to commit herself to them right now was overwhelming. Somehow she managed to resist, knowing they'd be aware she'd reached her decision for all the wrong reasons. Or, at that precise moment, for reasons that felt pretty damned right.

To avoid weakening, Chantal closed her eyes, riding the wave of her orgasm as Vilas's fingers explored her ass, creating a burning sensation that fused with her climax and pushed her completely over the edge. Release ripped its way through her body and she abandoned herself to it without inhibition, cresting the wave and clinging desperately until she could no longer prevent it from fading.

She collapsed against Rafe's chest in a sweaty heap afterward, breathing in the musky scent of his male arousal. He wrapped his arms around her and kissed the top of her head, almost chastely.

"Better?" he asked.

"No. It was good, but there was definitely something missing."

"Like our cocks?" Vilas suggested with a sexy wink, seating himself beside Rafe and taking Chantal's feet in his lap. "You know what you have to do about that."

"I almost did, but it would have been for the wrong reasons."

"We wouldn't have accepted you as our mate, not then," Vilas said.

"This is getting dangerously out of control." Rafe growled. "We never should have started this."

"But you did, and you're both erect again." Chantal slanted a flirtatious smile. "You do seem to be very…er, responsive."

It was Vilas who growled this time. "Talk about something else."

"I just wondered if you'd like me to help you out, that's all."

"You're enjoying this, aren't you?" Rafe asked, obviously trying not to groan.

"Just trying to make myself useful," she said sweetly.

"There's no need," Rafe said.

"Speak for yourself," Vilas said in an injured voice.

Rafe patted Chantal's butt and tipped her off their laps. "We'll get over it. While we get ourselves under control, I suggest you get yourself a shower. We can then go down and have dinner in the restaurant. It's date night, the start of our courting ritual."

"Aren't I supposed to work for a living?"

Vilas chuckled. "Oh, you will, never fear."

Chantal placed her hands on her hips and tried to look severe. They were playing games with her, but hadn't bothered to acquaint her with the rules first. Getting on her high horse when completely naked wasn't, she deduced from their amused expressions, easily achieved.

"I love it when you get mad, babe," Vilas said, blowing her a kiss.

Rafe winked. "Dress yourself up for us, darlin'."

Chapter Seven

Rafe and Vilas watched the sway of Chantal's slender hips as she left the room. The way her cute ass moved so provocatively had them both growling with renewed desire.

"Well," Rafe said, pushing a hand through his hair. "That's put any lingering doubts about her suitability as our mate well and truly to rest."

"She was well worth waiting for," Vilas agreed. "How long do you think it will take her to accept us as her mates?"

Rafe held out a warning hand. "We can't rush her, which is why we probably shouldn't have done what we just did to her. I hadn't intended to let things get to that stage, but—"

"But when she asked to see us fucking each other, it was only ever gonna end one way." Vilas grinned. "Admit it, man, from the moment you first saw her and knew she was the one for us, you've been as anxious to get your paws on that gorgeous body of hers as I have."

"Right, that was always gonna be a problem, but I had it under control."

Vilas let out a derisive purr. "Yeah, right!"

"I just hadn't anticipated her asking us to give her a show. As soon as we did, the sexy witch switched roles with us." Rafe threw his head back and growled. "I don't know about you, but I never really felt we were in proper control there. She always had the upper hand."

"She was curious because she'd never seen two men fucking before. Ask me, she hasn't seen or done much of anything in the sack."

"Good!"

"She enjoyed herself, though," Vilas said, rubbing the top of his head against Rafe's thigh. "Both watching and participating. That has to count for something. I don't reckon that rat Jack ever made her feel half so good about herself, even *with* penetration."

The hair on the back of Rafe's neck stood on end. "I don't want to think about anyone else penetrating our mate."

"Me neither." Vilas extended his claws and raked them through the space in front of him, as though attacking an invisible foe. "I was just saying."

"Once she's ours, there's a whole load of stuff we can get her to do, and she'll love it. I don't think she realizes just how sensual she actually is. But we mustn't try and persuade her *only* by taking her to bed. She needs to get a better handle on what we do here. How much more rewarding it can be than living completely in the human world."

"True, but Chantal has low self-esteem, the poor baby, so we owe it to her to make her see just how much she actually has going for her." Vilas grinned. "And if that means driving her crazy by giving her orgasms in all sorts of inventive ways that don't involve penetration, then—"

"Seems to me," Rafe said, rolling his eyes at Vilas's one-tracked mind, "that her brother has been the mainstay of her adult life."

"So we have to find him for her, and then offer to set her free if she wants to go back to her life with him."

"Right, but like I just said, in the meantime we need to give her a taste of what family life is like here in Impulse. She needs to experience belonging and being cherished just for being herself before she can make an informed decision."

"Yeah, I see what you're getting at." Vilas stretched out on a settee and extended his claws again to deal with a pesky itch on his belly. "Ah, that's better." His claws disappeared. "If she wants a dose of community living, where everyone looks out for everyone else, she's definitely come to the right place. Should we get some of the others to explain how things actually work?"

Rafe shook his head. "Best not be too obvious. Just let her mingle and ask questions as they occur to her."

"If she talks to some of the other human mates, they're probably the best ones to set her straight."

"Yep, that's what I reckon, too." Rafe rose from a prone position to his feet in one lithe movement, no deployment of limbs necessary. "I'm for the shower. We need to be ready to show our mate just how gallant and charming we can be." He grinned at Vilas. "So in your case, that might take a bit of work."

Vilas growled, slapping Rafe on the shoulder as they headed for their room. Laughing, Rafe leaned in and gave him a searing kiss.

"Let's shower together, buddy," he said. "Then perhaps we'll get through the evening without raging hard-ons."

"It's worth a try, I suppose, but speaking personally, the moment I'm anywhere near Chantal, my cock stands up and takes an avid interest. It doesn't seem to matter how often you and I screw, it still happens."

Rafe reached forward and cupped Vilas's balls. "Yeah, but don't forget that I love you, too."

"Jealous, sweetheart?"

"Nope, just reminding you who owns your ass."

"You're not worried that she'll come between us, surely?" Vilas wrapped a strong arm round Rafe's neck. "It'll never happen. There's plenty of room in this relationship for three of us."

"I love you, Vilas, even though you bug the hell out of me at times."

"Same goes for me." He growled. "Especially when you get those damned claws of yours on my sac. Geez, you've got me fucking rock hard again."

"I love you, but I'm already in love with Chantal as well, and it feels absolutely right."

"I'm *sooo* with you there." A rattling purr echoed in Vilas's throat as Rafe increased the pressure he was exerting on his balls. "You have my panther soul, big guy, and she has my human one."

"That sounds like a fair trade."

* * * *

"It's all very well telling me to dress up," Chantal muttered, "but I'm not exactly spoiled for choice here." Fresh from the shower, towels wrapped round her sensitized body and wet hair, she opened her closet door and rummaged through the few clothes she'd brought with her. "I came looking for my brother, not equipped with the right kit to go out on dates with predatory felines who seem to think they have some divine right to rule my world."

Not ready yet to examine her inadequate collection of clothes, Chantal flopped onto her bed and let the towel fall away from her body. She examined her nipples, still unable to account for the way Rafe had scratched at them with his vicious-looking claws and yet hadn't left a mark. She clutched one heavy mound of flesh and squeezed until the nipple poked between her fingers, frowning as she searched for telltale signs of Rafe's actions.

Nothing.

The rosy-pink peak was completely unblemished. It was so like it had never happened that Chantal could almost believe that she'd imagined it all.

Except, of course, she hadn't. Even her imagination wasn't that vivid. She spread her legs and touched her clit, still tender from the pounding it had received from Rafe's gorgeous cock. She was sopping-wet again, cream leaking from her vagina as she recalled the way she'd played with the boys—or rather, the way they'd played with her. She might have complained that the orgasm they gave her was inadequate, but that wasn't strictly true. It was a million times better than anything she'd experienced with Jack, mainly because he'd never given her a proper climax, the selfish bastard. She wouldn't tell them that, though. They were already quite disgustingly sure of themselves. Their egos didn't need any additional stroking from her.

Chantal wasn't sure who she was more angry with—Jack for being so self-centered, or herself for letting him get away with it for the entire two years of their one-sided relationship. Whatever happened to her here in Impulse, whatever decision she reached about her future, she had one thing to thank Rafe and Vilas for. They'd taught her that she didn't need to settle for second best. Nor would she, not ever again.

She'd been here for less than a day—a day that had turned her life on its head. If anyone had told her that she'd believe it when she was told she was in a town full of feline shape-shifters under virtual siege from other shifters, she'd have asked what mind-altering substances they were on. But she *did* believe it—hell, she'd seen the evidence firsthand—and was rooting for the cats to come through. She'd also enjoyed mind-blowing sex play with two hunky panther-men who seemed to think she was their mate for life. All that and the day wasn't even over yet. The fact that she wasn't running off screaming for help, and that she felt right at home here, probably meant she was as crazy as the felines.

"If they want a show, I'll give them one," she said aloud, grinning as she made up her mind what she'd wear for them.

Chantal owned just one dress. A flamboyant, emerald-green job that Jack had bought her—about the only gift she'd ever received from him, the tightfisted jerk—because he wanted her to attend some event at his college and make an impression. The dress was made of stretchy fabric, had a high neckline, and finished respectably a few inches above her knee, making a classy statement. Although it didn't reveal much bare flesh, it was so tight fitting that it left little to the imagination, fitting her like a second skin.

Chantal dried herself off and then pulled the dress over her head without bothering with underwear. Her tits were full but still firm and, standing sideways and examining her reflection critically in the full-length mirror, she had to admit that they looked pretty good beneath the dress. Her nipples pressed against the fabric, and she reckoned that the sight of them would drive the guys ever so slightly wild.

She wondered where this new, reckless Chantal had come from. Going out in public without underwear was something she'd never even have considered before today.

"Must be something in this damned thin air that's to blame," she muttered.

Chantal dried her hair, left it to fall where it liked, and applied makeup with a light hand. She slipped her feet into the only shoes she owned that weren't flat. They had four-inch heels and, teamed with her lack of underwear, made her feel as sexy as she'd privately always longed to be.

"Okay, let's go," she said to her reflection.

The guys both looked up when she reappeared in the lounge, smiles on their faces. Their gazes raked her body and those smiles turned into wide grins of approval. Imbued with renewed confidence, she gave them a twirl.

"Very nice!" Vilas said, sighing dramatically. "You're more like us that you realize, babe. We're not big on clothes, either."

"So I see." She laughed. They were both wearing stylish jeans and vests but, as yet, no shoes. She was willing to bet that, like her, they hadn't bothered with underwear.

"Come on then, sweetheart," Rafe said, slipping his feet into canvas shoes and proffering his arm. "Let's introduce you properly to some of the gang, now that you know what they really are."

Chantal made her way down the stairs, flanked by Rafe and Vilas. The bar was half-full, and Chantal recognized some of the faces from earlier. People smiled at them, some waved, and she caught a few admiring glances, presumably because of her dress. They headed straight for the restaurant, where Rochelle greeted them. She rubbed her cheek against Rafe's and Vilas's and then repeated the gesture with her. It felt incredibly soothing.

"I've saved you a booth at the back where you'll get some privacy," Rochelle said, her eyes sparkling as she led them to it herself.

"Thanks," Rafe said, sliding into the leather banquette and helping Chantal in after him. Vilas took up the position on her opposite side, sandwiching her between them, their knees touching beneath the table. "Bring us a bottle of the Pinot Noir Reserva while we look at the menus, please, Rochelle."

"Right away."

"You like wine?"

"Sure we do. We're as human as you are right now." Rafe smiled at her. "I should have asked you if you like red wine, or at least waited until you decided what to eat. I guess I kinda assumed—"

"That I'd have red meat? Perhaps I will this evening." She shrugged, feeling inexplicably carefree. "It must be something in the atmosphere that's gotten me so hungry."

"Sex always makes me ravenous," Vilas said, grinning at her.

Rafe rolled his eyes. "Which explains why he never stops eating."

"Ain't my fault if you can't keep your randy paws off me."

"Asshole!"

Chantal laughed at their easy banter. "Talking of the atmosphere, how come I struggle to breathe outside but am fine in here?"

"We control the airflow in buildings," Rafe explained. "Nothing magical about that. Just good, old-fashioned air-conditioning adapted to suit."

"We need visitors to feel comfortable some of the time," Vilas added.

"Yes, I wondered about that." Chantal took an appreciative sip of the excellent wine that had just been delivered to the table and paused to order beef stroganoff when Rochelle asked her what she'd like to eat. The guys both ordered double servings of veal chops.

"Good choice," Rochelle said. "I love our stroganoff, although since I make it myself, I probably shouldn't say so."

"I noticed you don't have many hotels here," Chantal said. "Given you have such a lovely beach, I thought that was strange."

"Mortals can't take the atmosphere for long," Vilas said. "Which is just the way we like it."

"So everyone who lives here is either a shifter or mated to one? Isn't that what you told me earlier?"

"Right," Rafe said, "but, for the reasons I also explained, numbers are low."

"Attacks and lack of mates, right?"

"Yep, but that was an observation." Chantal felt like she was drowning in the glorious depths of Rafe's vivid blue eyes as he focused them on her face and held her gaze. "I wasn't trying to put pressure on you."

"I believe you," she said softly, her insides melting with desire. She felt light-headed again, but this time it wasn't from lack of oxygen.

"Tell us more about your life," Rafe invited as they started on their appetizers.

"There's not much to tell. We were just a typical family. We didn't have a lot of money, but we were happy, or at least that's the way I remember it. Max said that he and I fought all the time." Chantal felt her euphoria dissipate as she recalled her childhood, before disaster struck and things were never the same again. "I was raised in Pittsburgh, Dad worked in the steel industry, Mom was a homemaker. She believed she was of more value being there for Max and me rather than trying to supplement Dad's income."

"Nothing wrong with that," Rafe said, squeezing her hand as though he understood her anguish. He was probably inside her head again.

"No, I think she secretly hankered after a career of her own, but Dad was old-fashioned about that sort of thing." She took a deep breath and another sip of her wine. "Then Dad got laid off when the steel industry fell into decline. He couldn't get anything else and resorted to doing any casual jobs that paid in cash. He'd been working all night as security at a club, came home and showered, then drove him and Mom straight to Max's graduation."

"It's okay, babe," Vilas said, taking her other hand. "Don't tell us if it upsets you too much to talk about it."

Rafe placed one hand on her knee and left it there. "We want to know everything there is to know about you, but we don't want to make you sad."

"No, I guess I should talk about it. I seldom do." And they were so easy to talk to, it felt kind of right to let it all out. "I was furious because I had a virus and couldn't go to see my big brother graduate. I've always wondered about that. I ought to have been in that car, you see, when Dad fell asleep at the wheel and wrapped it round a concrete barrier..."

"Hey." Rafe removed his hand from her knee, slipped his arm around her shoulder, and pulled her against him. "You can't go through your life feeling guilty for surviving. That's the last thing your mom and dad would have wanted."

"That's what Max always says." Chantal sniffed. "He's right, and so are you, but I can't help the way I feel."

"Things happen for a reason," Vilas said. "I find it helps if you think that way."

She offered him a wan smile. "Perhaps."

"And ever since then, you and Max have been everything to each other?" Rafe surmised.

"Exactly. That's why I know he wouldn't just disappear without telling me where he was going."

"And that's how we know the lions have him," Vilas said, snarling.

"They won't have killed him?" she asked anxiously.

"No," Rafe said, "almost certainly not. They won't hesitate to kill us here in Impulse to get their thieving paws on the place, but lions, despite their reputation, don't kill without a reason."

Relief washed through her. "Then you'll help me find him?"

"Count on it," Rafe said, rubbing his cheek against hers. "And, just so you know, there's no obligation on your part."

"We'll help because we want to."

"Helping people is what we do," Rafe added, "and we're pretty damned good at it, if I do say so myself."

"Modest, too," Vilas added, smirking.

"Thank you."

Chantal turned to Rafe, about to kiss his cheek. She changed her mind at the last moment and rubbed her cheek against his instead. Then she did the same thing to Vilas. The two guys smiled at one another over her head, looking like...well, like cats that had just gotten a whole vat of cream. By copying their marking gesture she'd obviously given them hope, causing Chantal to regret her spontaneity.

"Hmm, this is delicious," Chantal said to distract them, reverently forking stroganoff into her mouth and closing her eyes as it slipped down her throat.

Rochelle beamed. "You'll fit in here just fine, honey."

"You were going to teach me how to stop you reading my thoughts," Chantal reminded the guys when Rochelle left them alone again.

"Okay," Rafe said. "Close your eyes and think about me. Picture me in your mind. Are you doing it?" She nodded. "Right, now superimpose my face with something that makes you mad. Can you do that?"

"She'll be spoiled for choice," Vilas quipped.

"You're so full of it."

Vilas chuckled. "I aim to please, lover."

Chantal thought for a moment. What was guaranteed to raise her blood pressure? A slow smile spread across her face as she recalled Jack's expression when she caught him with his boss. That ought to do it.

"Yep, you're no longer my favorite person."

"Right, let's see if it works. Think about something, but keep that bad image of me in your head all the time."

Both he and Vilas went quiet for a moment. "Nope, you've tuned me out," Rafe said. "I've no idea what you're frowning about."

"She's thinking about whether or not to have dessert," Vilas said smugly.

"Same process, darlin'," Rafe said, shooting Vilas the finger. "But it'll be a whole lot easier this time because you have to put Vilas in a situation that makes you angry."

"Damn it," Vilas said a moment later. "Now I can't get a thing from her, either."

"How do I block you both at once?" she asked.

"She really doesn't want to let us in, does she?" Vilas said, pulling a face. "And we're such nice guys, too."

Chantal laughed. "A girl likes to have a few thoughts of her own."

"Just think of us both as bad guys simultaneously. That'll do it," Rafe said.

"Thanks, that shouldn't be too hard."

Rafe expelled a dramatic sigh. "She knows how to wound."

"How about that dessert, honey?" Vilas asked.

"Nope. It looks delicious, but I couldn't eat another thing." She smiled at them both, feeling more at home by the minute. "How do I communicate with you if I want to get your attention?"

"Just don't block us," they said together.

"If you become our mate, then you'll be able to do basic communication by pheromones."

Chantal offered them a cheeky grin. "What, I'll be able to read your thoughts for a change?"

"Hmm, possibly," Vilas replied. "It depends how receptive you are."

"You don't need to get inside Vilas's head to know what he's thinking about," Rafe said. "Sex is never off his mind."

Vilas reached across Chantal and squeezed Rafe's genitalia. "That's because you're such a phenomenal lover, big boy."

Chantal laughed. "Are you two ever serious?"

"Only when we have to be." Rafe looked up as someone loomed over their table. "What is it, Pascal?" he asked.

"Sorry to interrupt, Rafe, but it's Toby."

"I thought I felt a vibe," Vilas said, "but I was distracted and didn't pay it much attention."

"He's got her in here again?" Rafe asked, sighing.

"Yeah, you want us to deal with it?"

"No, I'll come." Rafe slid out of the booth. "Excuse me for a moment please, Chantal. Vilas will keep you amused, I'm sure."

* * * *

Vilas smiled at Chantal as Rafe walked away.

"What was that all about?" she asked.

"One of the young pumas has tried to smuggle a human in without permission." Vilas stretched. "He's done it before. The idiot ought to know he can't get anything past us. Just goes to show the power of *lurve.*"

"You have to have permission to bring someone into Impulse?" Vilas didn't like the way she frowned. "That sounds a bit like overcontrol."

Vilas laced his fingers with hers. "You have to understand that we're under constant threat of infiltration."

"Which is why you were suspicious of me."

"Right. Toby met this girl locally and thinks he's in love, but she absolutely wouldn't make him a good mate."

She pulled an indignant face. "Why should you be the one the judge?"

"Not me, babe, but the council as a whole. Apart from anything else, this girl has a large family living locally. It wouldn't be possible for her to keep our secret." He sighed. "A lot of the youngsters forget about the rules, especially when they've been living as humans for a while."

"Why does Rafe have to be involved? Can't the pumas sort it between themselves?" Chantal shook her head. "I can't believe I just said that. I'm talking about pumas sorting their own problems like it was totally normal."

"You'll be surprised how quickly you'll get used to it. And to answer your question, Rafe is the boss. He needs to get involved in important stuff like this."

"You and he are alpha panthers, that much I get…I think. But how does that give him authority over everyone else?"

"He's colony leader." Vilas shrugged. "Rafe is head and shoulders the best cat to keep us all in order, but don't you dare tell him I said so."

Chantal smiled. "You love him, don't you?"

"Why wouldn't I? He saved my life."

"Really? How did that happen?"

"Maybe not my life, but my sanity. He made me understand what I was supposed to be." Vilas shared the last of the wine between their two glasses. "My earliest memories are of being shuttled between foster homes, you see."

"You never knew your family?" Chantal touched his knee. "That's really sad. I might have lost my parents too soon, but at least I had their loving care when I was small."

"It was pretty bad for me when I was a kid because I never felt like the others. And when you're different, kids pick up on it and can be pretty cruel."

"You didn't know you were a shifter?"

"No, but I had these feelings that I soon learned not to talk about because everyone thought I was crazy. I know now that they were my feline instincts trying to come out. That's also why I know it would be living hell if we lose our power and I can no longer shift." He clapped a hand over his mouth. "Oh shit, forget I said that. I'm not supposed to put any pressure on you."

"Said what?"

"Atagirl." The hand that had covered his mouth slid to her knee and crept beneath the hem of her dress. She gasped when he flicked his thumb across her naked pussy, just once, and then withdrew it, grinning smugly. "Thought so," he said.

"So, you were telling me how Vilas saved your life."

"I came to Impulse on a school field trip when I was about twelve. All the other kids complained about shortage of breath, but the moment we crossed the bridge I felt like I'd been reborn."

"You'd found where you were supposed to be."

"Right. Rafe knew I was here, of course. He somehow separated me from the rest of the group and talked to me for ages. He was only sixteen at the time although, of course, that would actually be forty-eight in your years."

Chantal wrinkled her brow. "This is getting complicated."

"You're forgetting what we told you earlier. Shifters only live three years to your one in places like Impulse because of the special ions in the air. They're becoming fewer and farther apart with changes in weather patterns. That's another reason why the lions and bears wanna get their thieving paws on Impulse."

"So they can triple their life span and increase their numbers?"

"Yep." He leaned over and kissed her lips, lapping at the corners of her mouth with his tongue until she mewed with pleasure. "You're so goddamned perfect that I can't stop looking at you, but I didn't say that, either."

Chantal laughed. "Go on. I want to know more."

"A lot of us are sent to school in the human world, so we age at the same rate as our human classmates, and get the same education. Mikael went to med school before he came back to Impulse. Shifters can and do live quite comfortably in the human world, they just don't get the longer life span that we enjoy here in Impulse. Anyway, I felt drawn toward Rafe the moment I laid eyes on him. He explained to me what it was about me that made me so different, and then it all started to make sense. Some of the elders in the colony wiped my existence from the human records so I wasn't missed, and I've been here ever since."

"What happened to your family?"

"We're not sure. Some shifters were culled back about the time I was born. Humans got it into their heads that we existed because a couple of shifters got careless and were seen by hunters, who pursued them. That started a real hue and cry. People were afraid of us because they were ignorant—"

"A bit like medieval witch hunts."

"We're guessing that my parents were amongst those that were killed. No one knew what I really was so I was put into the care system. I was disruptive because I sensed I didn't belong, and so no family held on to me for long."

"Until Rafe saved you." Chantal reached up to touch his face. "No wonder you love him so much."

"He and some of the others taught me how to shift, which is when I really started to feel at home. Rafe and I worked our way up through the pecking order, and when Rafe's father retired, he and I took his place as alpha males. A year or two later Rafe was elected as overall colony alpha, and the rest, as they say, is history in the making."

"Rafe takes his duties very seriously, doesn't he?"

"We all do. Every member of the colony is important. We look out for each other, and if anyone's in trouble, we all help out. I'd die for Rafe, he'd do the same for me, *and* we'd both do the same for you, in a heartbeat." He grinned. "No pressure, babe."

"Sorry about that." They both looked up and Vilas realized he'd been so engrossed that for once he hadn't sensed Rafe's return.

"All sorted?" Vilas asked.

Rafe shrugged. "The girl's been sent home. She won't remember anything. Pascal's trying to talk some sense into Toby."

Vilas rolled his eyes. "Good luck with that."

"Right. Anyway, hope I'm not interrupting anything," Rafe said with a knowing wink for Chantal.

"Would it matter if you were?" Vilas complained.

"Not in the slightest." He held out a hand to Chantal. "Come on, darlin', let's go and mix with the others in the bar. You need to get to know a few people, and we promise not to have them influence you in our favor."

Chapter Eight

"As if you'd do such a thing!" Chantal teased.

"I'm serious," Rafe said. "If you decide to say, it won't be through collective coercion. But there's one thing you do need to know before you make up your mind. Vilas and I were talking while you got ready, and we're both agreed that we're falling in love with you."

"Not because you can save us," Vilas added, serious for once.

"But because you're you."

"We sensed your oneness with us before you even got here. Don't suppose you can feel it the way we do, at least not yet, but you will."

Chantal felt tears spring to her eyes. No one other than Max had admitted to loving her in her entire adult life. The guys weren't playing with her mind when they said it. They were being completely honest with her. She didn't know how she could be so sure of that, she just was. She was tempted to tell them that, in spite of her efforts to remain objective, she was falling for them as well. She resisted—it was way too soon to raise their hopes when she hadn't actually made up her mind. She'd been too quick to trust in the past, too anxious to grasp at anything that made her feel cherished, without bothering to ask the right questions. This time she needed to be absolutely sure she knew what she wanted.

"Thank you." She rose up on her toes to kiss each of them in turn. "I promise I'll make up my mind soon. I realize how important it is to you. It's just that—"

"Shush!" Rafe placed a finger against her lips. "This is a big deal for you. Vilas and I will survive until you decide. And if you decide against us, we'll survive that, too."

"Probably," Vilas said, grinning at her as he patted her butt.

As soon as they returned to the bar, Vilas's attention was caught by someone, leaving Rafe to introduce Chantal to some of his fellow shifters and their mates. Then he faded away and left her to chat with them alone. She admired that about both her would-be mates. They could have used that intimate dinner setting, with low candlelight and soft music, to talk some more about their sexual exploits that afternoon. She was pretty sure that would have kept her in a near-permanent state of arousal, helping to convince her that Impulse was the place for her. The way she felt right now, vulnerable yet safe and protected, she wouldn't have taken much persuading. Instead, apart from the odd slip from Vilas, it seemed they were doing all they could to let her make up her own mind.

Mikael cast an appreciative smile her way. "I'm glad you made it here at last," he said. "Rafe and Vilas had almost given up on you." Before she could put him straight on that, he spoke again. "What do you think so far? It's pretty overwhelming, I guess. A lot to take in."

"Yes." She returned his smile, thinking that his dark blond, stripy hair was so tigerish that it was obvious, now she knew he was a shifter, what species he must be. "Is it true what Rafe told me, about your cures for childhood illnesses, I mean?"

"Yeah," said another guy, also with stripy hair, who prowled up to Mikael and placed a hand casually on his arm. "I'm Philo," he said, extending his other hand, "Mikael's fellow alpha tiger. Pleased to meet you."

"Likewise."

"Yes, we do run the clinic and help where we can," Mikael said, making their remarkable achievements sound like no big deal. "Before I even graduated med school I'd decided that modern medicine had a lot wrong with it. So I fell back on some of my granddad's herbal knowledge, teamed up with Philo, who's a Botanist, and decided that between us we couldn't do any worse than the so-called experts do."

"It gives us a buzz to do some good in this tarnished world of ours," Philo added.

"I'm sure it must do. If I can help at all while I'm here—"

"We'll find you something to do, don't worry about that."

"Yes, but I don't know how long I'll be here for, so don't plan too far ahead."

Mikael and Philo exchanged a glance that implied they knew better than she did, but they didn't contradict her.

People, shifters, whatever, came up to chat with her, putting her more and more at ease as the evening progressed. She noticed things about them that she hadn't seen when working the bar that morning, perhaps because they'd been careful to shield her from their feline tendencies on that occasion. Now that she knew what they were, they didn't seem to feel the need to keep their claws sheathed, or to hide their lithe abilities. One guy was lying flat out on his stomach across an open window, legs and arms hanging down on either side of it, looking entirely comfortable as only cats can in such circumstances.

"I know exactly how you feel," an attractive woman said to her as she caught Chantal staring at the guy hanging over the window frame. "It takes some getting used to, and they do so like to show off. Still, you'd be surprised how quickly it becomes the norm."

"You're human, I take it."

"Yes, I'm Lily, mated with those two over there," she said, pointing to a couple of guys having a lively debate on the opposite side of the bar. "They love each other to death but seem to enjoy arguing." She rolled her eyes. "Go figure. If they haven't got me in bed, I spend my time playing referee."

"Rafe and Vilas seem a bit that way."

"Goes with the territory, honey. My guys are beta panthers so I know about what I speak."

"Er, do your two...um—"

"Fuck each other?" Lily shrugged. "Sure. That's all they did until I came along and made things a bit more interesting for them."

"Well, if I stay—"

"What do you mean *if?*" asked another woman who Chantal thought was called Irena. "You've got the chance of having those two hunks all to yourself. Why would you walk away from that?"

"Irena!" Lily said, with obviously feigned shock. "You're mated."

"So?" Irena shrugged nonchalantly. "That doesn't mean I've been struck blind."

The three of them laughed together, leaving Chantal with an intense feeling of well-being. This strange collection of people really did seem to care deeply for one another, like the family she longed to be a part of. And she could be. All she had to do was say the word. In less than twenty-four hours, Rafe and Vilas had come to be the focal point of her world, there was no escaping that fact. They were weakening rapidly, but it was within her ability to right that situation. In order to do so, she'd have to have sex with them, of course. Not that making such a mega sacrifice would influence her thinking, of course!

"What if someone not in the colony comes in?" Chantal asked Lily. "Wouldn't they notice something strange about the way you all behave in here?"

"We'd know before they got beyond the parking lot," Irena answered for Lily. "Not that many strangers venture this far from their hotels—"

"Because of the atmosphere?"

"Right. This place tends to be the colony's unofficial headquarters. We can be ourselves here most of the time."

"So I see." Chantal nodded toward a man on the opposite side of the bar who had whiskers sprouting from the side of his face that looked a bit like an electrified moustache. A woman had draped herself round him and was pulling the whiskers gently through her fingers. Chantal could hear the man's deep rumbling purr even above all the noise in the bar.

"Oh, he's a young jaguar showing off to Sally-Anne," Irena said dismissively. "They've only just been mated and can't keep their paws to themselves."

"A cat's whiskers are especially sensitive," Lily explained.

"A feline erogenous zone," Irena added, rolling her eyes. "Take it from one who knows."

"Hence the name of this place, I suppose." Chantal smiled. "Is that why they like to rub faces with one another?"

"Pretty much, yeah."

Rafe materialized at her side. "Some of us are going up to the apartment," he said softly. "I've called a council meeting to decide what to do about your brother."

"Oh, then I'll come and—"

"No, it's just for the council at this point. I'll fill you in on what we decide later. You stay here and enjoy yourself. Lily and Irena will take care of you. Come up when you're ready."

He rubbed his cheek against hers and was gone. She watched as Mikael and Philo followed him from the room.

"Those two behind Mikael are Vadim and Zayd, alpha jaguars," Lily told her.

"That's Kane and Tyronne next in line, the alpha leopards," Irena added. "And the pumas, Pascal and Kai, are bringing up the rear."

"Well," said Lily, handing her glass across the bar for a refill. "Now we've got all that testosterone out of the way, we girls can have some fun."

But in spite of Lily's best efforts to get a party going, a lot of the young shifters drifted away.

"They have to patrol," Lily explained. "We're vulnerable to attack right now."

"Because of me," Chantal said bleakly.

"No, honey," Irena said. "It goes with the territory, literally."

Chantal asked a lot of questions and enjoyed getting to know Lily and Irena. What she was reluctant to admit, even to herself, was that the bar seemed empty without Rafe and Vilas filling the space with their vibrant presence. She must be tired, she decided. It had been a very long, very strange day.

"You're going to have to excuse me, ladies," she said, hiding a yawn behind her hand. "I need to get some rest."

"We understand," Lily and Irena said, sharing an amused glance. "We're about to leave ourselves."

"Have fun up there," Lily said, waving her fingers at Chantal.

"Don't do anything I wouldn't do," Irena added with a smug smile.

"Which means you get to do just about anything you like," Lily said, linking her arm through Irena's and heading for the door.

"Do you need me to help you clear up, Stefan?" Chantal asked the young man tending the bar.

"No, love, I've got it covered. You get yourself upstairs now."

"Night then," she said, yawning again as she left him to it.

A tingling of anticipation swept through Chantal as she climbed the stairs, simply because she'd get to see Rafe and Vilas again. So much for not being needy, she thought with a wry smile. She was unsurprised when she opened the door to the sitting room and all the men gathered round the table were already looking her way. Of course they knew she was coming, and not just because they'd heard her footsteps on the stairs.

"I didn't mean to interrupt," she said. "I just need to get some sleep."

"We're about finished here, anyway," Rafe said.

The sound of chairs scraping on the wooden floor confirmed his words. All the other council members wished her good night and headed for the stairs. She was left alone with Rafe and Vilas.

"Did you have a good time down there?" Rafe asked.

"Yes, Lily and Irena are lively company."

"They lead their mates in a merry dance, just like you will us, sugar, if you decide to stay."

"Vilas!" Rafe chided. "No pressure, remember."

"Just sayin'," Vilas protested a little too innocently.

"What did you decide tonight?" Chantal asked, taking one of the vacated seats at the table and studying the map spread across it. "Impulse is just a long peninsula, isn't it?"

"Yes," Rafe said. "That makes it easier and harder to defend."

"It's easy to defend from the land because the only way in by road is across the one bridge," Vilas explained, "or on foot along the beach."

"But you're vulnerable on all sides by water," she said.

"Yes. Not so much on the gulf side, because the beach shelves and there aren't many places to bring a boat in," Rafe explained.

"That doesn't stop them diving in and trying to swim it."

"Big cats can swim?" Chantal shook her head. "I thought you didn't like water."

"It's not our preferred method of getting about, but desperate times and all that," Vilas said. "What the lions do, the sneaky bastards, is to send their best swimmers in human mode and get them to try and make it to shore."

"They haven't managed it yet. We've always been able to fend them off," Rafe said, raking a hand through his unruly hair. "Our problems lie on the Intracoastal side, where there are places absolutely everywhere to stop boats."

"I can see that. But what did you decide about Max?" she asked. "I don't want you putting the colony in danger for my sake."

"We're sending out scouts tonight to see what news we can pick up," Rafe said.

"Shifters like to gossip just as much as humans," Vilas added.

"You're going yourselves, aren't you?" Chantal felt overwhelmingly concerned for their safety.

"We go out every night," Rafe said softly. "It's what we do."

"Please don't take any unnecessary risks. Your powers are so weak."

Rafe lifted her from her chair and into his lap. "Don't worry about us, baby. We'll be fine."

He stood up and carried her through to her room, Vilas at his heels. Once they got there, he put her down and she stood obediently while he pulled her dress over her head. Both men sucked in sharp breaths when she stood before them naked. Vilas ran a hand across one of her breasts, causing the nipple to pebble and throb. Rafe merely looked at her like he never wanted to tear his gaze away.

"We have to go," he said with a heavy sigh. "Get to bed and rest. You'll be perfectly safe here, and we'll talk in the morning. We might know more by then."

Each of them bent to kiss her and then left the room. Chantal wanted to go after them and beg them to stay, but when she tried to move, her feet appeared to be rooted to the spot. A moment later she heard the window in their adjoining room swing open and knew she was too late. They were gone and she'd never felt so alone in her entire life.

Chantal washed, brushed her teeth, and climbed into bed, bone weary but unable to sleep. The way she saw it, this colony of complete strangers was putting its collective lives on the line for her brother. She'd never be able to live with herself if a single one of them received so much as a scratch, but there didn't appear to be any way to stop them. It wasn't her fault. She accepted that she'd been used but still felt responsible. The sensible thing would be to leave. That way they wouldn't feel the need to protect her, and Impulse wouldn't be under threat because of her. Max wasn't here, so she had no reason to stay.

The only problem with that master plan was that the thought of leaving Rafe and Vilas tore at her heartstrings, causing her acute physical pain. She believed them when they told her she was the only mate for them and that by letting them fuck her she could restore their power. She was falling in love with them, damn it, otherwise she wouldn't feel so uneasy at the thought of them being out there, weak and vulnerable to attack.

Was it possible to fall in love within the space of a single day? Apparently so, because that was what Chantal felt for them, no question. Her insides roiled as she seriously contemplated committing herself to them. For life. But if she did that, they would never stop looking for Max. They might be stronger, but they'd still be putting themselves in danger.

There had to be another way.

She could agree to be their mate, have sex with them to restore their power and *then* leave. They'd said mating was for life, no divorce allowed. But if they weren't officially married, divorce didn't come into it. As far as she could tell, having sex with each of them just once would be enough to give them back the power they'd lost. She could block her thoughts from them so they wouldn't know she planned to leave. Even if they picked up the vibes, short of physically restraining her, they had no way of forcing her to stay.

For their sakes, she'd do what it broke her heart to even contemplate. She had finally found not one but two men whom she could love absolutely, and who loved her in return. Instead of the happily ever after life she'd dreamed of for years, she would make the ultimate sacrifice instead, all in the name of love.

She would sleep with them, and then disappear from their lives forever.

Presumably, the lions would know what she'd done and release Max without anyone getting hurt.

It was a perfect plan, Chantal decided, as she cried herself to sleep.

Chapter Nine

The sun was up when Chantal woke. That surprised her because she didn't think she'd slept at all. Her gut churned when she recalled what she had to do, the sacrifice she had to make for the sake of the colony as a whole. She stifled a cry of regret, feeling hollow inside, and just for a moment her resolve wobbled. There had to be a way to stay with the guys *and* keep them safe.

"Get real," she muttered.

She got so damned mad when she reflected upon life's habit of toying with her. It seemed to enjoy fooling her into thinking she had some elusive right to happiness, waiting until she was hooked before kicking her in the teeth. She'd finally found two men who fulfilled her wildest dreams, but if she stayed with them she'd be the cause of their downfall. You simply didn't do that to the people you loved, and that was all there was to it. She'd get out of their lives, start again somewhere else, and somehow find the will to survive.

She pulled a T-shirt over her naked body, slipped from her room, and peeped round the guys' door, just to make sure they'd gotten back safely. She'd intended to remain awake until she heard them return, but physical and emotional exhaustion had obviously put an end to that plan.

Her heart lurched when she discovered that their room was empty, the bed neatly made, no sign of recent occupation. It was still early, and they'd told her that after their nights on the prowl they slept most of the morning away. So where were they? Her emotional system went into overload, and she felt on the edge of hysteria. She was too late to save them. The lions must have somehow gotten to them. Something bad had happened to them—she just knew it.

What to do? Someone must know what had gone wrong and be making plans to get them back. She'd go down to the bar and offer to help—if it wasn't too late for that. Chantal refused to allow that thought to take hold. She absolutely had to stay positive. Dashing into the living room, not looking where she was going, she ran headlong into a solid brick wall. A brick wall that had rock-hard abs, impossibly broad shoulders, piercing blue eyes, and a familiar musky scent.

"Hey." Rafe's hands came to rest on her shoulders. "What's wrong?"

She glanced up at him and Vilas standing beside him, and burst into tears. Rafe sat down, pulled her onto his lap, and cradled her head against his chest. Vilas sat beside him, grabbed her legs, and rested her feet on his thighs, gently massaging their soles. Chantal couldn't stop bawling, but the guys didn't seem to mind. Vilas continued to rub her feet. Rafe's large hand swept her back with smooth, reassuring strokes, and they didn't say a word until she got herself under control.

"I...I thought you hadn't come home," she said, gulping back fresh tears. "Your room was empty. I thought you'd been hurt. I...I couldn't bear the guilt."

"Why would you feel guilty?" Vilas asked.

"It's my fault. I came here and—"

"I told you nothing would happen to us," Rafe said softly. "We're indestructible."

"Don't say such things. It's bad luck."

"We love it that you care," Vilas told her.

"I do care," she said reluctantly. "I wish I didn't, it would make things so much easier, but I do."

"You're tired. You can't be sure—"

"What are you doing up so early?"

"It's gone eleven," Vilas said, amused. "Even we tend to surface by then."

"It can't be that late." Chantal shook her head. "I'm supposed to work this morning."

"It's okay. Stefan has it covered," Rafe said. "We figured you'd need to sleep late after the emotional upheavals of yesterday."

"You're so thoughtful," she said, nipping at Rafe's shoulder because she couldn't think how else to express herself.

"All part of the service, ma'am."

"Talking of servicing," she said, taking a deep breath and sitting up straighter so she could look at them both at the same time. "I've decided to take you up on your offer. If you still want me, I'll be your mate."

"You're kidding me!" Vilas jumped to his feet, extended his claws, and punched the air with them.

"Baby, you know we want you, but we need to know that you love us both," Rafe said, rubbing his cheek down the side of her face. "It's too soon for you to be absolutely sure. You're tired and overwrought. This isn't a decision that can be made on a whim."

Chantal slithered from his knee and stood above Rafe, hands on hips. "Don't you dare tell me how I feel, Rafe Landon! Even if you think you can read my mind, I still know it better than you ever will. It doesn't take more than a second to fall in love, and," she added in a more moderate tone, "I think I fell for you both the moment I first saw you."

"That's good enough or me," Vilas said, swooping in for a kiss. "It's about time someone other than me stood up to Rafe."

"You really mean it, don't you, babe?" Rafe sent her a scorching gaze. "You're absolutely sure? Because there'll be no going back once we're mated."

Her insides melted as she met his gaze and held it. If only that were true! "Do you want to stand here debating the issue, or would you rather introduce me to that vacant space in your bed you've been keeping warm for so long?"

Rafe let out an elongated whoop, swept her into his arms, and carried her through to their room.

"Send out a pheromone," he said to Vilas, "and tell everyone to organize the party to end all parties to welcome our mate to Impulse."

"Already on it," Vilas said, grinning as he stepped out of his jeans, the only item of clothing he appeared to be wearing. "I'll see to that while you prepare our mate for the ceremony."

"What ceremony?" she asked, worried now that they hadn't told her everything. She didn't want to sign any binding contract if she was going to walk away.

"This needs to be official," Rafe said in full alpha-male mode.

Chantal watched him as he moved about the room with such lithe coordination—beautiful, graceful, and yet unquestionably virile and male—that she wanted to weep with regret. He really was an alpha in every respect of the word, and the entire colony appeared to accept his authority. If Chantal could stay, she'd have made sure she stood up to him. As Vilas had said earlier, no one except him ever did. She forced all thoughts of leaving from her head, frightened that they'd pick up on them. She'd put her heart and soul into restoring their power first, hoping that would involve more than one mating session. Better safe than sorry! It would be her reward for the broken heart that awaited her round the next corner.

"Welcome, sweet darling," Rafe said softly, pulling the T-shirt over her head and casting it aside. He stepped out of his jeans and stood in front of her, his cock rock hard. It jutted thick and angry, reaching almost all the way up his navel. Damn it, he was well proportioned, but she'd accommodate that gorgeous thing or die trying! "There's a small ritual we need to perform that will bind you to us."

"Bind me how?" she asked, showing more anxiety than she'd intended. "No one mentioned anything about binding before."

Vilas came to stand beside Rafe, also fully erect and ready for action. "It's our equivalent of a marriage ceremony," he said.

"Kneel in front of us, Chantal, and bow your head." She did so, feeling slightly uneasy but powerless to resist their authority. "Do you swear by all that you hold most sacred to be our mate, true only to us, for the rest of your days?"

Chantal nodded.

"You have to say that you do, darlin'."

"I do," she muttered, crossing her fingers behind her back.

"We love you, Chantal Lake, and pledge our lives to keeping you safe and happy."

They each placed a hand on top of her head and the strangest thing happened. She felt a bolt like a mild electric current pass from their hands to consume her entire body. She trembled as it took hold and coiled itself deep in her gut, making her feel as though a missing part of her had just woken from a long sleep. She blossomed like a flower spreading its petals for the first time—rejuvenated, feminine, completely and totally in tune with her innermost self in a way she'd never before realized was possible.

"What did you just do?" she asked, blinking up at them.

Rafe extended a hand, pulling her to her feet and into his arms. "Welcome, babe, we love you."

He reached behind him and picked up a square velvet box. When he opened it, something bright twinkled up at her. She gasped when he picked up a collar that looked as though it was studded with diamonds and fastened it round her neck.

"Now you really belong to us," he said. "It was my mother's, and I've waited a long time to see it round my own mate's neck."

Geez, how could she possibly walk away now? "I saw some of the other ladies wearing collars in the bar last night."

Vilas nodded. "Given to them by their men to show they're mated."

"You're mated to the leader of the colony and his alpha so you get to wear diamonds."

Rafe kissed her deeply, his long panther tongue delving into her mouth and sending a kaleidoscope of wild sensations streaking through her body. Passion ignited as he deepened the kiss and his hands wandered to her ass, pulling it hard against his erection.

"What do you want me to do to you, Chantal?" he asked when he broke the kiss.

"I want you to fuck me," she said brazenly, meeting his gaze. "And then I want Vilas to fuck me as well."

"Then you must kneel before us again and ask us nicely."

Chantal scrambled back to her knees and lowered her head. "I have needs, masters," she said, seeming to know what they wanted to hear. "Needs that only the two of you can satisfy."

"Have you been good?" Rafe asked.

Hell, this is fun! "No, master. Please show me how to be good."

"Stand up, Chantal. Go to the corner of the room and face the wall."

She did as they asked, sensing that they were communicating with those damned pheromones of theirs as she stood there with her head lowered, feeling the full focus of their gazes on her ass. It was *sooo* unfair. She wanted to know what they were talking about. She'd ask them to teach her—except there wouldn't be enough time before she left. The stark truth hit her like a punch in the gut and her legs almost buckled with the force of her regret.

"All right, Chantal, you can come back now."

She walked toward them, keeping her eyes lowered, biting her lip to stop herself from smiling.

"Go and lay in the center of the bed, darlin'," Rafe said.

Chantal made herself comfortable, anticipation roiling through her, and noticed that Vilas was wielding a camera.

"Wedding day pictures," he said. "Spread your legs for me, babe, I don't wanna miss the good bits."

Chantal laughed, put at ease by Vilas's infectious enthusiasm. She wondered how a man with such a raging hard-on could prance round a room with a camera without losing his momentum. Somehow she wasn't surprised when Rafe pulled her arms above her head and attached them to the headboard with fluffy restraints.

"You have to do as we tell you, babe," he said. "We're in charge here."

"You mean the only way two great big men like you can control a little thing like me is by using restraints?" Chantal opened her eyes wide in mock surprise. "If this gets out your reputations will never recover."

Vilas roared with laughter. "She's gonna be quite a handful, Rafe. I can see that already."

Chantal died a little, so wishing she'd be around for long enough to make that true.

Rafe chuckled. "She has an independent streak that she hasn't learned to quell yet. We're gonna have to teach her some discipline."

Chantal rather liked that sound of that. "Would you mind too much fucking me first?" She closed her legs and rubbed her thighs together. "I'm kinda damp down there and it's getting uncomfortable."

The guys seemed to find her desperation amusing. "I've waited more than half a century to hear my mate utter those immortal words," Rafe said.

* * * *

Rafe lay full length beside his precious mate and extended the claw on his right index finger. He half expected Chantal to be frightened by the sight of it, but he should have known his feisty mate was made of sterner stuff. Rather than fear, her expression conveyed anticipation, curiosity, but most of all, impatience. She would need to be taught patience—but not today. Rafe was barely in control of himself, so he could hardly chastise Chantal for stepping out of line.

Vilas was on her other side, now focusing a video camera on Chantal's delectable body. Rafe ran a hand possessively down the entire length of her, marking his territory, causing Chantal to quiver beneath his touch. She was so sensitive, so responsive, so eager, that she stole his breath away. God, but he wanted her! All the sacrifices he'd made over the years for the good of the colony had been leading up to this blissful moment. At times he'd ranted against the hand life had dealt him. Why did he have to be the alpha? Why did he have so much responsibility for the welfare of the colony? Other male shifters sometimes risked mating outside the loop with no discernible effect on their powers. He simply didn't dare to risk it.

Now he knew the waiting had been for a purpose. Chantal was everything he'd hoped for in a mate, and more, and he'd keep her safe for their rest of their days or willingly die in the attempt.

"If you think my tongue turns you on, babe, just you wait until you see where I can put this," he said, waggling his claw at her.

She pushed her lower torso toward it. "All I seem to be doing right now is waiting," she said pensively. "Who does a girl have to kill to get fucked in this colony?"

"Well, now, let's see what we can do about that, shall we?"

Rafe kissed and licked his way across her lips and down the long column of her neck, lapping at the pulse beating out of control at the base of her neck. She struggled against the restraints, moaning softly as he teased her into a heightened state of awareness. His tongue rasped over one of her solid nipples and she cried out.

"She's so fucking needy," Vilas said, zooming in with the camera.

"Yeah, she is. What do you want from me, Chantal?"

Chantal moistened her lips. "Please," she moaned. "I need to feel you inside me."

"Turn over, darlin'. The restraints swiveled. Rest your weight on your elbows and get up on your knees for me."

Vilas and Rafe exchanged an appreciative glance at the sight of her pert ass sticking skyward and her tits swinging invitingly beneath her.

"You gonna get her started?" Vilas pheromoned.

Rafe grinned. *"If I don't you sure as hell will."*

"You got that right, buddy."

Rafe leaned over Chantal from behind, running his tongue down the length of her spine and massaging a heavy breast with one hand. Prurient noises slipped from her lips and she wiggled her butt at him like she knew what was coming and wasn't prepared to wait.

"Patience!" Rafe purred the word against the back of her neck and gently nipped at it. "Everything comes to those who wait."

"She's got cream sliding down her thighs," Vilas said, zooming in to get a better shot of her flowing juices.

"Hmm, so she has."

Rafe pushed her legs wider apart and bent his head, applying this tongue softly to the inside of her thighs, drinking in her juices more reverently than if they were the finest vintage wine. To Rafe, that's precisely what they were—sweet, fragrant, and headily addictive. He teased her by extending his tongue and flicking it across her cunt, just once. It was enough to make her scream his name.

"Rafe, don't made me beg," she gasped.

"Bit late for that," Vilas observed, grinning as he continued to record events for posterity.

"Okay, babe, I hear you."

Rafe laved the cheeks of her ass with his tongue, before tracing its crack and rimming her anus. She tensed, and then sighed.

"Relax, darlin', and let me love you like you deserve to be loved."

Vilas threw a tube of lube to Rafe. He caught it one-handed and smeared a generous amount over her crack. She squealed.

"That's cool."

"Hmm, and you look so fucking hot with lube all over your backside, darlin'." He inserted one finger, struggling to get it past her tight muscle. "Stop fighting me, Chantal." He leaned forward and placed kisses across her lower back. "You trust me, don't you?"

She nodded. "You know I do."

"Then let me in. You'll love it when you get used to the sensation."

He could sense her trying to relax, gauged when she'd done so, and slid his finger a little deeper.

"It burns."

"Give it a moment." He felt her closing about his finger, showing just what a quick study she was. "How does it feel now?"

"Better. Very sensitive." She turned her head sideways and looked up at him from beneath her curtain of hair. "It's kinda nice when you move your finger. The sensation, you know."

"Oh, I know." Rafe added another finger, distracting her by pinching one nipple as he did so. "There, you're a natural at this."

She wiggled against his fingers. "I'm so glad you're doing this to me."

Rafe rattled a deep purr against her neck. "You and me both, darlin'."

He reached out to Vilas again and took the butt plug he held out to him. Removing his fingers, he quickly lubed the toy, and before Chantal had a chance to realize that he'd upped the game, he pushed it gently into her anus. She tensed up.

"What's that?"

"It's a plug, sweetheart. It'll distend you so that when we want to fuck your ass later, you'll be able to accommodate us. How does it feel?"

She tossed her head backward, seemingly contemplating her response. "Intrusive, but in a pleasant sort of way. I guess it'll take some getting used to."

"That's the idea."

Rafe slid his index finger claw between her legs and, very gently, agitated her clit with it. She gasped, pushing herself against it, so intent upon the sensations he was creating that she didn't seem to notice that he'd pushed the plug into her ass so far that it slid all the way home.

"Turn over again, babe."

Vilas set the camera on a tripod at the end of the bed and resumed his position beside Chantal. Once she was on her back again, Rafe balanced himself over her, holding his weight on his arms.

"Spread your legs for me, darlin', and let me love you good."

"How does the plug feel?" Vilas asked, running a hand lazily down her thigh.

"Actually, it feels red hot."

"It's filled with oil. Your body heats it up and it…well, I guess you can feel what it does to you," Rafe said. "I'm gonna fuck your cunt with the plug still up your ass. Then you'll know what to expect when Vilas and I take you together."

She mangled her lower lip between her teeth. "Is that what you plan to do?"

"Not right now."

"Spoilsport!"

Vilas chuckled. "She's hot for us, man."

"Yeah, but she needs to get used to the idea first. We don't want to hurt her."

"Don't I get any say in this?"

"No!" they said together.

"Bend your knees up, sweetheart," Rafe said.

As soon as she did so, Rafe gently parted her creamy folds and slid three fingers inside her channel, delving and probing as his thumb swept across her clit. Vilas reached behind her and pushed the butt plug a little deeper. It was all it took for her to scream Rafe's name and buck to a climax against his fingers.

"Naughty!" Rafe tapped her backside hard. "No one gave you permission to come."

"Sorry." Her voice was a strangled moan. "I'm so damned hot that I couldn't hold it. It's your fault. That plug is setting me on fire."

Rafe chuckled. "As it's your wedding day, we'll allow you to get away with being disobedient just this once, Mrs. Landon-Tanner."

"Mrs. Landon-Tanner? Hmm, I like the idea of that."

"How about my wedding present to you? Do you like the idea of that, too?"

She glanced down at his throbbing cock and the corners of her lips lifted into a sensual smile. "Yes, please!"

"Geez!"

Vilas took his own rigid tool in hand and gently massaged it. Rafe slid the head of his between the lips of Chantal's pussy, closing his eyes and sighing as, finally, after all these years of waiting, he was on the point of penetrating a woman. *The* only woman he would ever mate with. She was slick, and tight, and so fucking inviting that he almost lost his mind, and his load, then and there.

He tried to think about something else—anything to dispel the overwhelming need he felt to possess her. There would never be another first time and so it needed to be special. Hell, it *was* special for him—the culmination of all those years of sacrifice and frustration. Rafe's objective was to make it special for her, too. She'd been with men before, damn it, and knew what to expect, but Rafe didn't want to think about her previous lovers. He's go out of his mind with jealousy if he did. Instead he would concentrate on making sure she never wanted any other men, other than him and Vilas, for the rest of her days.

He thrust a little deeper, groaning as his sensitized cock finally found its only real home. The little witch closed the walls of her cunt around him as she welcomed him inside, lifting her hips to drive him deeper. Rafe was conscious of Vilas's hand on his ass, two fingers pushing inside. With his panther flexibility, Vilas also bent his head to Chantal's tit so he could suckle and chew on her solid nipple. Rafe knew he'd be using his teeth, getting her used to being tormented with the light pain they both so enjoyed. He wanted to feel a part of this momentous occasion, as he should. Rafe purred loudly to show his approval as he drove himself deeper inside their mate, filling her to capacity with his desire and the all-consuming love he felt for her, showing her with deeds rather than words that he was totally committed to their future together.

"How does it feel?" Vilas asked.

"Heavenly," Rafe and Chantal said together.

"Put your legs over my shoulders, babe," Rafe said. "I wanna go deeper."

"I feel like you're tearing me apart," she said as she wiggled into position.

"I'm hurting you?"

"No," she moaned. "You're driving me insane. Fuck me, Rafe. I really need you to fill me completely."

"Babe, you'll be the death of me yet."

Chantal tensed at his words, causing Rafe to wonder what he'd said. He desperately wanted to prolong the moment by teasing her. In the face of her unbridled enthusiasm he was powerless to hold back. He thrust into her as hard as he could because he could sense that the last thing she wanted was to be treated gently. She effortlessly consumed his entire cock deep inside her tight pussy, thrashing her head from side to side on the pillows. Her eyes were alight with passion and a modicum of desperation. She moved with him as he set up a steady rhythm, heady sensations consuming him as the momentum built.

Vilas had released his own cock but still suckled her nipple. His other hand disappeared beneath Chantal, presumably to push the ass plug a little deeper.

"You're being fucked by two cocks now, darlin'," Rafe said, aware of perspiration breaking out across his brow as he struggled to hold back. "How does it feel?"

"Like I never want it to stop. That thing in my ass feels so goddamned hot."

"What about Rafe's huge cock fucking your cunt?" Vilas asked, lifting his mouth from her nipple.

"It all feels so incredible. Don't stop biting me, Vilas. I love it. I'm gonna come again. I can't stop it."

"We'll come together," Rafe said, picking up the pace. "Stay with me, babe. This is gonna get rough."

"Rough it what I live for."

Rafe hammered himself into her, conscious of her tightening about him even more, her breath coming in shorter and shorter gasps.

"That's it, darlin', now we're fucking. You feel my cock deep inside you. It's all for you, baby. Take what you need from it. When I'm inside you I feel like I could conquer the fucking world. We were meant to be together, sweetheart, and now we'll never be apart again."

"Rafe, I'm coming. Vilas, push that damned thing in further. Both of you, I'm coming for you now."

She screamed both their names and milked Rafe's cock like she thought she'd never get the chance to do so again. Rafe stayed with her, watching her face as she fragmented, emotion and tenderness tugging at him on a level he was powerless to control. As soon as he sensed her orgasm fading, he renewed his thrusts and let himself go.

"Hey, baby, I'm gonna come."

Vilas's fingers had returned to his ass. At least three of them were buried inside his anus as he fucked a woman for the first time in his ninety-odd years and his alpha partner finger-fucked his ass. He exploded deep inside Chantal with a strangled oath, following it up with a string of filthy words. His stream of semen appeared to go on indefinitely as Rafe, in an elevated state of sensory overload, rode his orgasm like a dying man. Chantal screamed, closed around him, and came again.

When they both stopped pulsating they collapsed on their backs, panting and grinning, kissing and laughing. Vilas kissed them both and lay on Chantal's opposite side, one arm thrown possessively over her and Rafe.

"When do I get my turn?" he asked.

Chapter Ten

"Right now, lover boy," Chantal said, leaning awkwardly up so she could kiss him, her movements hampered because her hands were still shackled above her head.

Vilas grinned and pulled her into his arms, full of love and admiration for the way that she'd adapted to their methods so quickly. He kissed her like he never wanted to stop, sweeping her lips with the tip of his tongue and then pushing it deep inside her mouth. Her lips were warm and mobile as they fused with his, the incendiary nature of her response blowing both his mind and his fragile control.

Resting on his side, his erection lay hard across her thigh, twitching almost painfully with need. Watching her and Rafe fucking each other's brains out was such a turn-on that he'd almost lost it. Somehow he'd held it together, but knew he couldn't last for much longer. Rafe reached across and stroked his cock, in tune with his needs, as always.

"You like it when I bite your nipples, sugar?" Vilas asked when he broke the kiss.

"Yes, I didn't realize that pain could be such a powerful aphrodisiac."

"Well, in that case…" Vilas grinned at Rafe. "Fetch me a paddle, man. We're gonna give our mate her first lesson in discipline. Turn over, babe. Get up on your knees for me and let me at that sweet ass of yours."

Vilas occupied his time alternately kissing, nipping at, and lightly spanking Chantal's buttocks until Rafe returned with the paddle.

"You like me spanking you, darlin'?"

"It tingles. It's like that plug up my backside burns harder when you hit me."

Rafe chuckled. "That's kinda the idea."

"Your ass sure does look pretty when it's all pink from a spanking," Vilas said, sitting back on his haunches to admire his handiwork. "Let's see if we can improve on that, though. Go with the pain, darlin'. When I spank you, just relax into it if you can and wait for it to transmute to pleasure."

"How do you know that it will?"

He and Rafe both purred with amusement. "It will, honey," Rafe said. "You're so damned responsive that this sort of stuff has to have been invented with you in mind."

Vilas extended one claw and barely touched Chantal's clit with it. At the same time he brought the paddle down lightly on her butt. She cried out, then craned her neck sideways and smiled at him.

"Like that, babe?"

"Hmm, I'm not sure." Her eyes danced with a combination of devilment and passion. "You'd better do it again so I can decide."

Rafe laughed. "It's one greedy little cat we've got ourselves here, buddy."

"Yeah, but she was made for us."

"No arguments there."

This time, when Vilas spanked her, Rafe did the same thing to Vilas, using a switch. Vilas almost *did* shoot his load this time. He loved it when Rafe punished him, but he hadn't been expecting it and had been taken off guard. Chantal squirmed and Vilas spanked her a little harder, digging deeper into her swollen clit as he did so.

"You're making me crazy, Vilas," she moaned, tossing her head from side to side. "And I love it."

"I know you do, babe, but you're not supposed to admit it." Vilas rubbed his cheek against her ass and purred. "It's meant to be a punishment."

She shot him a sideways, somnolent smile. "Then punish me some more."

"Those that ask don't get, sugar," he said, removing his claw from her nub and waggling it at her instead.

"She's ready for you," Rafe purred in Vilas's ear. "Just like I'm ready for you."

"We're all gonna fuck together," Vilas said to Chantal. "Move onto your back again, darlin', spread your legs for me, and let me at your gorgeous cunt."

As soon as she was in position, Vilas's fingers disappeared inside her, buried as far as they'd go. She pushed against them, moaning softly. Rafe dropped the head of his cock against her lips and she sucked it into her mouth, her eyes sparkling with mischief, presumably because she was running her tongue across his glans.

"I thought you were saving that for me," Vilas said in an aggrieved tone.

"Just getting it warmed up for you, buddy."

"Vilas, I need you," Chantal breathed, pushing harder against his fingers.

"What, my fingers and that plug up your ass aren't enough for you?"

"Not nearly."

Vilas pretended to be annoyed as he positioned himself between her legs, removed his fingers, and inched the head of his cock into her.

"Christ!" he breathed. "She's so fucking tight. I think I've died and gone to heaven."

He felt the mattress shift as Rafe positioned himself behind him and lubed Vilas's anus.

"Rafe's gonna fuck my ass while I take your cunt, Chantal," Vilas explained. "Next time the three of us do this, you'll be the one in the middle."

"Just imagine that, babe," Rafe purred as he slid into Vilas's backside. "Our two cocks fucking you senseless. You think you might like that?"

She let out a dreamy sigh. "I can't wait."

"Open your legs as wide as they'll go, darlin', and keep perfectly still. Let Rafe and me do all the work."

"For someone who's never had a woman before," Chantal said, panting with expectation, "you sure know how to turn one on."

"We've had enough time to think about it," Vilas replied.

He smiled as he worked his way a little deeper into her, inch by inch, savoring every glorious moment as his cock was enveloped within her warm wetness. He teased her by withdrawing and then plunging a little deeper with his next thrust. The feel of Rafe working his ass spurred him on. This was like nothing he'd ever known before and he was all out of patience. He drove himself savagely into Chantal, slapping the side of her buttock with one hand.

"That's it, babe, you've got it all now. You've taken every goddamned inch of me, you greedy little she-cat."

"You're enormous, Vilas. I'm going to explode."

"Rafe's enormous, too. He's filling my ass and I'm loving having you both. Hell, I love you both to distraction. Now come on, let's really fuck each other."

Vilas and Rafe moved together in perfect harmony. They'd done this to each other, or something like it, virtually every day for years and knew exactly what floated one another's boat. They moved savagely, Rafe's loaded balls slapping against Vilas's ass in time with the sound of his hand spanking the side of Chantal's butt.

"Pick it up, lover," he said to Rafe, his voice tight with tension, "I can't hold out much longer."

"Let's all come together," Rafe said breathlessly. "Come on, babe. Are you close?"

"Yes, fuck it, yes! Give it to me, Vilas. Make me come for you right now."

She closed about him, screaming as her orgasm hit. Vilas and Rafe didn't falter, moving faster and faster, sweating and swearing as they, too, reached the pinnacle.

"That's it, darlin'," Vilas said. "You've got me now. I'm all yours."

He yelled to the rafters as he shot his load deep inside his mate, his cock twitching and pulsating as relief flooded through him and finally, after years of waiting, he felt completely at peace. Rafe, predictably, remained rock hard inside his ass, ignoring both him and Chantal as they reached noisy climaxes. Presumably sensing that Vilas was spent, he picked up the pace.

"What do you say, buddy? Shall we try and give her another one?"

Rafe was more than capable of bringing Vilas to a plateau again almost immediately and Vilas rose to the occasion, in all respects. He lowered his head to feast on one of Chantal's nipples as he hardened inside her again. She opened her eyes wide, clearly astonished to feel him come back to life so quickly.

"Come on, darlin', stay with me. I've got another one for you."

"I can feel it." She lifted her hips and sucked him in a little deeper. "I love it that you recover so quickly."

"When you get to have Rafe's huge cock up your ass, you'll understand how that can happen."

"I can't wait, and I'm as hot as hell, Vilas. I need to come again."

He and Rafe, turned on by her words, moved faster than before, delving deep, satiated by their recent climaxes and ready to make this one last.

"Move with us, babe," Vilas said. "But make sure you keep to our tempo."

Fire exploded inside Vilas as their mate did as he asked. The most unimaginable spangles of pleasure stirred deep within his gut and radiated slowly toward his outermost reaches. Rafe's balls were so hard they were almost painful when they slapped against him. Vilas didn't care. He lived for that sort of pain, and for the pleasure he knew he was giving to the man he loved. He pushed his ass farther toward him, and then retreated to thrust as hard into Chantal's tight channel as he could manage.

"Boys, fuck me!" Chantal screamed. "I can't believe what you're doing to me. What you're making me feel. I'm on sensual overload."

"Believe it, sweetheart," Rafe said, his voice tight from the strain of holding back. "This is what you're in for every day from now on."

"Will it always be this explosive?"

"Hell, this is nothing," Vilas said. "You just wait and see what we've got lined up for you, once you get used to taking us both."

"You have plans for me already?"

"We've had plenty of time to plan what we intend to do to our mate."

"And tried it out on each other?"

"Some of it. We wouldn't want to disappoint you." Vilas lowered his head and bit hard on one of her nipples. "Now, let it go, babe. Feel us fucking you and enjoy."

She screamed as she closed about his cock, pulling him over the edge with her. Rafe gave it up, too, gushing into his ass just as Vilas shot his heavy load into Chantal. He screwed his eyes tight shut as he reveled in the fire that lanced through his veins and the overwhelming love he felt for the two people who'd just given him the most intensely satisfying orgasm of his entire life.

* * * *

Chantal, totally exhausted, turned on her side, rested her head on Vilas's chest, and expelled a deep sigh of contentment. Was life allowed to be this good? No, of course it wasn't, but she refused to think about what she had to do very soon. Rafe released her hands, extracted the plug from her butt, and spooned himself against her back, half-erect again, she couldn't help noticing. These two were insatiable.

"Do you feel your power being restored to you yet, boys?" she asked.

Rafe purred out a laugh. "Give us a moment."

"It's just that if you don't, we could always repeat the process." She flashed a cheeky grin. "I wouldn't want you getting all weak and feeble on me."

"Told you," Vilas said, admiration in his tone as he ran his fingers gently through her hair. "She's obsessed with our cocks."

"I'm obsessed!" She half sat up, her tits bouncing against her chest, causing Rafe to reach out and cup one. "That's good coming from you two."

"We've been celibate for decades," Vilas protested. "So we have an excuse."

"Not exactly."

"We need to get you spruced up," Rafe said. "We can do this again later, but right now we have a wedding party to attend."

"Our wedding party," Vilas reminded her. "And the whole colony will want to celebrate with us."

"Not to mention envying us like hell."

Reluctantly Chantal allowed her somnolent self to be levered from the bed and carried to their enormous bathroom. Vilas filled the oversized circular tub to the brim with steaming water and poured half a jar of fragrant essence into it. Rafe helped her into the bath and joined her there. Vilas fiddled with something on the wall and then joined them as well. She looked up as a screen sprang to life, showing the video Vilas had taken of her and Rafe fucking.

"Wow!" was all she could think of to say, glad that the water hid the fact that her juices were flowing freely again.

A hand sought out one of her tits and squeezed. A hand on her other side zoomed in on her cunt. They sat in silence, watching their performance as Rafe played with her nipples and Vilas brought her to a screaming orgasm with his fingers. As soon as it abated, Rafe flipped her over so that she was kneeling on the padded seat and gripping the handrail on the edge of the bath. He slipped into her from behind, filling her to capacity as he fucked her in time to the rhythm the three of them were setting on the video.

They climbed from the bath when the water turned cold and the video ran out. Vilas wrapped her in a fluffy towel and carried her back to the bedroom. It seemed she wouldn't be allowed to walk anywhere when these two were around. She died a little inside when she remembered that she wouldn't be here for long enough to find out if that was actually true. While Vilas dried her off, Rafe went into the sitting room, returning with a hanging rail full of beautiful dresses.

"Where on earth did they come from?"

"Irena runs the dress shop in town. We asked her to send a few things over for you to choose from for tonight."

"You didn't need to do that."

"You're our mate." Vilas growled. "You think we won't dress you right?"

"I know, but…" She couldn't explain the guilt she felt, didn't want to alert their hypersensitive minds to her turmoil, and so she enthused over the dresses instead. "What do you think of this one?" she asked, holding a black chiffon number against her.

"Not black, honey," Rafe said. "This is a wedding."

"How about this one then?" She extracted a vibrant, blue, floaty creation, the color almost identical to her men's eyes.

"Yes," they said, nodding in unison.

There were shoes to go with each dress, making Chantal feel like a complete fraud. It didn't take her long to get ready. She retreated to her own room to apply her makeup and when she returned to the sitting room, Rafe and Vilas were waiting for her, both looking devastating in white tuxedos. They were even wearing proper shoes in honor of the occasion. She gulped as she stared at them, wondering if she was completely insane to walk out on them. Then she remembered the alternative and knew the only way she could repay their love was to give them up, even if the pain of separation killed her. Better she died than they did. There was nothing special about her, but they were unique, irreplaceable.

Instead of cashing in on their powers, the colony was doing so much good without letting anyone know it. They didn't need money or public acclaim. They just had the common decency to do the right thing.

Somehow she had to find the strength to emulate their example.

"Ready, Mrs. Landon-Tanner?" Rafe proffered his arm.

"Absolutely, let's do it."

She entered the bar flanked by her two mates and barely recognized the place.

"Oh!" She felt giddy with pleasure as she took in the colorful decorations, the party streamers and the sparkling fairy lights. The overwhelming perfume given off by dozens of fragrant flower arrangements and the scented candles that appeared to occupy every surface made her gasp with delight. The place was packed with beaming colony members, all of them clapping and cheering when the three of them walked in. Rice was thrown at them, people came up to rub their faces, and everyone made a big fuss over Chantal.

"Glad you made the right decision," Lily said, hugging her. "You won't regret it."

Irena flashed a knowing grin. "You look like a lady who's just been thoroughly fucked."

Chantal put on a bored expression, which probably didn't fool anyone. "It's part of my duties, apparently."

Irena hooted with laughter. "That's what my guys keep telling me."

"Do they ever get less demanding?"

"Nope," Lily and Irena said together.

"Good!"

"Lovely collar," Lily said, touching it with the tips of her fingers. "It suits you."

The girls were soon separated as others came up to claim Chantal. The booze flowed freely, a table groaned under the weight of the food that Rochelle and her helpers had somehow cooked up in no time flat, and everyone appeared to be in a party mood. Even so, Chantal noticed lots of the males coming and going. Rafe clearly wasn't letting his guard down. She reminded herself that such a high state of alert wouldn't be necessary if it wasn't for her, but refused to dwell upon her regrets. This party was for her and it was impossible not to be swept up by the prevailing mood of optimism.

A band played in one corner of the room. Chantal was already starting to recognize faces. She was sure that was a puma playing a hauntingly beautiful melody on the trombone, and wasn't that one of the young tigers scraping a bow across a violin?

"Care to dance, Mrs. Landon-Tanner?" Rafe asked, wrapping his arms round her waist from behind.

The floor cleared and everyone applauded as Rafe swung her into his arms. His breath peppered her face and his hands clasped her ass, pulling her against his hard-on. No one seemed to think that the slightest bit strange. Swept up by the mood, Chantal shamelessly rubbed herself against his length. Rafe dropped his head and captured her lips in a drugging kiss as they swayed to the music, feet barely moving, virtually fucking in front of over a hundred people.

"Do you know what I'd like to do to you right now?" he murmured in her ear.

"No, tell me."

"My turn." Vilas tapped Rafe on the shoulder and took his place.

"You'll have to be punished for that later," Vilas whispered.

"For what?" Chantal asked, raising a brow in innocent query.

"I saw you making a show of yourself, rubbing up against Rafe's cock."

"It's well worth rubbing against."

"Even so."

"If I'm going to be punished, I might as well make it worthwhile."

Chantal pushed her groin against Vilas's hard length, laughing when he groaned aloud. Others had joined them on the floor now and Chantal decided she'd better behave herself.

"Later," Vilas said, wagging a finger beneath her nose as Mikael took his place and swung her into an energetic salsa. He was a great dancer and Chantal loved to dance.

"I'm glad you're here," Mikael said to her. "You've already worked wonders for Rafe and Vilas."

"That obvious, is it?"

"Honey, when you've waited as long as those two have to get laid, it doesn't take a rocket scientist to figure out what the three of you have been doing all day."

Chantal blushed. "Is there anyone here tonight who *doesn't* know?"

Mikael shook his head. "I doubt it."

"Oh hell!"

Chantal was sorry when full darkness fell and the party started to break up.

"I suppose you two are off out for the night."

Chantal tried to suppress her disappointment as she linked arms with her two mates. The thought of slipping away while they were gone made her feel like the worst kind of jerk, especially after the party the colony had just thrown for her. She reminded herself that she'd done what she'd set out to do. She'd restored their power and there was no point in prolonging the agony.

"Are you kidding me?" Rafe looked at her like she'd taken leave of her senses.

"This is our wedding night," Vilas reminded her, like she needed any reminding.

"Vadim's got security covered tonight," Rafe said, "leaving us free to cover you."

Chantal didn't know if she was more ecstatic or desolate. Of course she wanted to spend the night with them, but each time she so much as touched either one of them, she fell a little more in love with them both. Having them for an entire night would make it even harder for her to leave them tomorrow.

"What are we waiting for then?" she asked, somehow managing to summon up a bright smile, even though her heart was breaking.

Chapter Eleven

Chantal felt a little tipsy as the guys escorted back upstairs. She must have had more champagne than she'd realized. She wasn't a big drinker and it had gone straight to her head.

"Hey, steady there." Rafe caught her in his strong arms when she missed her step. "Don't want you hurting yourself."

"Whoops!" She giggled and swayed against him.

Vilas laughed. "Our mate seems to have enjoyed the party a bit too much."

"I did...hic, really I did." She flashed a smile at each of them, but their features seemed a little blurred. Must be the dim lighting, she supposed. "There's one thing I don't understand, though," she said when they reached the sitting room.

"What's that, honey?" Rafe asked.

Chantal kicked off her shoes, sighed with relief when her toes started to regain some feeling in them, and curled up in the corner of a sofa with her feet tucked beneath her. "Well, Irena and Lily both have two mates."

"Right."

"But some of the others I spoke to only have one, while some seem to have three." She frowned. "What's the norm?"

Rafe shrugged. "There is none. Vilas and I always knew we would share our mate because we've been together for so long—"

"And you love each other and wouldn't want to be separated." Chantal nodded. "I get that bit."

"Those with one partner are usually mated to another shifter early on in their lives," Vilas explained.

"I see." She canted her head and blinked but still couldn't get them into clear focus. "And those with three or more?"

"Like us, they grew up together, waiting for the right mate."

"What about Rochelle then? I know you said she's a lynx. Is she waiting for a human mate?"

Rafe shook his head, his expression somber. "Rochelle was mated to another lynx. He was killed about a year ago when the bears took us by surprise with a raid."

"Oh no, how terrible!"

"Rafe was damned near killed in another attack," Vilas said, touching his buddy's arm and scowling at the memory.

"That slash across your belly?" Chantal asked.

"Yeah, but it's better now, thanks to Mikael."

"Like hell it is!" Vilas growled. "You'd just better not get it ripped open again."

"I wasn't planning to. Mikael's cures are miraculous, but they hurt like a bitch."

"Rochelle's cooking is really good," Chantal said hastily, not wanting to think about Rafe getting injured. "Can she look for another lynx to mate with, or does she have to live out her life alone?" Chantal sniffed, feeling suddenly like she was on emotional overload. Rochelle having to live out her life alone seemed like the saddest thing in the world. Perhaps that was because Chantal was feeling sorry for herself. She would have to do the same thing if she wanted to keep her mates safe. "That seems such a waste."

"She can mate again if she wants to," Rafe said. "With either a lynx or a human. The same rules don't apply to female shifters."

Chantal rolled her eyes, propelled out of her momentary self-pity by Rafe's chauvinistic-sounding comment. "Of course they don't!"

"She hasn't shown any indication of wanting anyone else," Vilas added. "It's probably too soon."

"She looked so alone tonight." Chantal wiped a tear from the corner of her eye. "Everyone else seemed to be paired off and she just stood on the sidelines, watching but not joining in."

"Don't let it upset you, babe." Rafe crouched beside her and caught another tear with his forefinger. "Shit happens, but Rochelle will recover in time."

"She hasn't met another mate who's right for her yet," Vilas said. "Hopefully that will happen."

"Anyway," Rafe said, kissing the top of her head as though she was a small child. "You're not allowed to be sad. This is your wedding day, remember."

Like I can forget. How many brides walk out on their grooms on the very first day? "Yeah," she said, stretching her arms above her head. "So what happens now?"

Their responding chuckles were decidedly wicked. "Are you sober enough for anything to happen?" Rafe asked.

"Sure I am."

Rafe laughed. "Okay then, stand up and prove it. See if you can walk to the other side of the room and back again without falling over."

"I love it when you get all authoritative on me," Chantal said, blowing him a kiss as she sprang to her feet with an agility that belied her supposedly drunken state. Sitting down had made the world stop spinning and she could see them clearly again. That wasn't such a good thing. She realized now that she'd probably drunk as much as she had to blot out the pain of separation, but it didn't seem to have worked. She was sober again and the pain hadn't gone anywhere. She tripped lightly across the room without wobbling, returned to where the guys were standing and offered them an extravagant bow. "See," she said triumphantly. "Stober as a dudge," she said, deliberately slurring and mispronouncing her words. "When do I get my prize?"

"You'll do," Rafe said, an anticipatory grin gracing his beautiful face as he patted her backside.

He and Vilas sat themselves on the sofa she'd just vacated, leaving her standing in front of them. They were in dominant mode again and she knew better than to move a muscle without their permission.

"Take your clothes off for us, Chantal," Rafe said, focusing his eyes on her with unnerving stillness.

Chantal didn't have much to take off—just the dress and her underwear. Even so, she'd do her damnedest to give them a show. First off she took the pins from her hair, slowly shook her head, and it tumbled down her back in a tangle of disorderly curls. Her dress came next. She managed to unzip it without help and let it fall from her shoulders in what she hoped was a tantalizing fashion.

They hadn't seen the only decent set of matching underwear that she owned and wore with the dress—a black gauze bra with a colorful edge around the cups and matching thong. Her nipples hardened as she lowered the dress, letting it go completely so that it pooled around her feet with a soft whooshing sound. The guys both sighed, clearly liking what they saw, filling her with the impulse to tease them a bit more. She stepped away from the ruinously expensive dress, leaving it where it had fallen, and danced around the room in her flimsy underwear. Chantal felt drunk again, drunk on the power she wielded over these two as they watched her with avid fascination. Judging by the bulges tenting their pants, they were as anxious to get down to business as she was, but they had to catch her first.

"Come back here and take your bra off, Chantal."

Rafe's voice was rife with authority and, much as she wanted to continue taunting them, she was powerless to disobey. When her bra fell away, she threw it aside with reckless abandon and cupped her breasts with her hands, figuring they'd like to see her play with herself. Rafe inhaled sharply.

"The thong, too," he said curtly.

Chantal stepped out of it, twirled it around her index finger like a sling, and threw it at them. Vilas caught it and, laughing, put it in his pocket.

"We've got something for you to put on for us," Rafe said when she was wearing nothing except her diamond collar and an anticipatory smile. "Come here."

"Am I allowed to ask what it is?"

All those leather straps and metal rings looked a bit weird to Chantal, but she didn't hesitate to let them put it on her. The leather webbing harness crisscrossed her torso and left her tits poking out through the gaps. One strap fixed to the top and held up the flimsy bottom half that resembled the pants of a bikini, except nothing covered her pussy or the crack in her ass.

Neither guy answered her question, busying themselves instead with tightening straps until she was trussed up to their satisfaction. They'd both kicked off their shoes, she noticed, but apart from that they were still fully dressed, whereas she appeared to be wearing some sort of fetish outfit. It was hugely arousing to see the appreciation in their eyes and her pussy throbbed almost painfully as she waited for one of them to touch her. Please God let them touch her before she disgraced herself again and her pussy leaked all over the place.

"Are you comfortable?" Vilas asked.

"Yes, but I'd still like to know what it is."

"It's called doraphilia," Rafe said. "Arousal from touching skin, hair, leather, or fur."

"Well, I guess that works for you guys, given your circumstances."

"And you look gorgeous in it," Vilas told her. "All those lovely soft curves…yum. How do you feel?"

"Sexy," she said, not stopping to even think about it. "I love the way you're both looking at me."

"And we love you, babe," Rafe said, "but we're not finished yet."

As though on cue they fell to their knees on either side of her and laved her nipples with their mobile panther tongues. Chantal threw back her head, closed her eyes, and squirmed as wild sensations hit her from all angles. Being dressed like this and having these two touching one of her most sensitive places with nothing more than their tongues was enough to make her dizzy all over again. But this time her light-headedness had nothing to do with the amount of wine she'd drunk. She placed a hand on top of each of their heads, needing the support to stop her legs from buckling when they began nipping at her tits with enough force to send liquid fever coursing through her veins.

"Guys, perhaps we can—"

"She can take it," Rafe said, nodding to Vilas.

Take what?

Vilas released her nipple and crossed the room, returning with what looked like a couple of clamps connected by a chain.

"They're nipple clamps," Rafe told her. "Ever tried them before?"

"No, but I've heard about them."

"They restrict the blood flow to your nipples and make them even more sensitive." Rafe grinned at her. "Vilas and I wear cock rings sometimes, which have the same effect on our pricks."

"You'll look sensational wearing these clamps with the leather harness," Vilas said. "Will you do it for us?"

"My wedding present to you both?" Chantal smiled. "Bring it on, boys!"

The guys shared a feral grin as they carefully lubed her areolas and attached the clamps.

"Comfortable?" Vilas asked.

"It feels lovely," she said. "What's the chain for?"

"It's weighted," Rafe explained. "If we tug on it, it'll increase the pressure."

"Can I play with your nipples, both of you, before we fuck?"

"Would that turn you on, babe?"

She nodded, unable to explain that she wanted to try and make *them* lose control for a change. "You both have such muscular chests," she said instead. "It'd be fun exploring."

"Sounds good to me," Rafe said, an unholy light in his eyes.

Vilas scooped her into his arms and carried her into the bedroom. By the time he'd deposited her on the bed, Rafe was already naked. It didn't take Vilas two seconds to follow his example. Vilas landed on one side of her with a soft thud and an anticipatory purr rattling against the roof of his mouth. Rafe, the crazy show-off, leapt from the floor and landed on her opposite side, covering more than ten feet with the featherlight coordination of a cat. He lay flat on his back and grinned at her, pure predatory male as he tugged lightly on the chain connecting the nipple clamps, causing surges of sensation to ripple through her in mind-blowing waves.

"Feel free to play with us any time you're ready."

He clearly thought that he got to go first. She offered him a seraphic smile and then turned her back on him to run her fingers playfully over Vilas's chest. Vilas roared with laughter.

"I think you've just been insulted, man," he said. "Oh geez!" he added when Chantal bent her head and grazed one of his nipples with her teeth.

Chantal was conscious of Rafe's breath on the back of her neck and his fingers caressing her butt as she leaned over Vilas. Without acknowledging Rafe, she took tiny nips at first one of Vilas's nipples and then the other, slowly working her lips down his torso until she reached his rigid cock.

"That's it, baby," he said, holding its base and guiding it into her mouth. "Suck it with those sweet lips of yours. Ah, Chantal," he sighed as she drew her tongue across its head and licked away the drop of pre-cum that sprang from it. "Keep doing that, darlin', and I'll be creaming your throat in no time flat."

When Chantal felt Rafe's finger rimming her anus, she instinctively tensed up. He tapped her butt and then dropped a line of hot kisses across both buttocks.

"Relax, babe," he said in a persuasive whisper. "You're so goddamned sexy in that harness that you're driving us both nuts. What you need to do now is put your trust in me enough to let me in."

Vilas pulled out of her mouth, snaked an arm round her waist, and tumbled her on top of him.

"Rest your weight on my shoulders, Chantal, and straddle me on your knees," he said. "Stick your butt in the air and let the man do his work."

This was it then. They really did intend to take her at the same time. She was glad. At least she'd experience the feeling just once before she had to leave them. The memory would have to sustain her for the rest of her days because after this Chantal knew that she wouldn't let any other men touch her. Like Rochelle, she would end her days alone. Better to be a has-been than a never-was, she thought with a wry smile, more determined than ever to make the most of what was happening to her now.

"What's wrong?" Vilas asked anxiously. "If you don't want to do this, just say the word. No pressure, we promise."

Damn, she'd let her guard down and Vilas had sensed her despondency, read her mind, or whatever. "If you dare to stop then I won't be responsible for my actions," she said with enough conviction to let them think she was serious. Hell, she *was* deadly serious.

Rafe's wicked laugh echoed round the room. "I think she's up for it," he said.

She felt cool lube squirting over her ass and then Rafe's fingers made a fresh assault on her anus. At the same time Vilas reached for one of her breasts, dangling just above his face, and licked the tingling nipple. The pleasure that spangled through her made her shiver, and she barely noticed when Rafe pushed his fingers—more than one, she felt sure—a little deeper.

"Rock your body back against my hand," he said, tapping her butt to regain her attention. "See how it feels."

"Oh!"

She sensed the two men sharing a smug glance. "Oh indeed," Vilas echoed. "We did try to tell you."

"It's amazing," she said dazedly. "I had no idea."

"I'm not hurting you?"

"No. It burned a little at first, but now it feels absolutely sublime."

Vilas reached down and parted her folds before placing one hand on her hip and guiding her onto the head of his cock. She didn't want to go slowly and sank down fast, even though Rafe still had his fingers in her backside."

"Ah!" she said this time, wondering how it was that her vocabulary had suddenly become so limited.

"That's it, sweet darlin'," Vilas said, releasing a heavy breath. "Take it all into that tight pussy of yours and let me love you good."

Rafe withdrew his fingers, replacing them with what had to be the tip of his cock. Chantal tensed. He was enormous and, despite his assurances to the contrary, she was convinced it would never fit.

"Let me in, babe," Rafe said, peppering kisses down the length of her spine, his hot breath against her damp skin making her shiver.

Vilas moved lazily inside her, with what felt like a claw agitating her clit, an effective means of distraction. When Rafe tried again she felt him slip past her tight muscle and waited for the pain that didn't materialize. She relaxed and he slipped in another inch.

"There you go," he said softly. "Now you've almost got us both. That's what you want, isn't it, darlin'? You want our cocks to fuck you every which way possible."

"Yes," she said breathlessly. "But you're too big. You'll never—"

Vilas regained her attention by playing with her aching nipples. Rafe slid in a little deeper, and then deeper still. She felt stretched to capacity, but nothing could have prepared her for the reality of two thick cocks pressing deep inside her. Dangerously close to orgasm, she wanted time to stand still, for all the problems she'd caused for Rafe and the colony to dissipate. She wanted for them to be able to do this forever.

It was never going to happen. Mentally Chantal railed against the unfairness of life. Why had she been given this opportunity, only for it to be snatched away from her again? Given her time over, she'd have preferred to live in ignorance.

"It feels so damned good, boys," she said on an agonized moan. "I don't know if I should move, or keep still, or—"

"Don't move a muscle, darlin'," Rafe said, rasping the back of her neck with his long tongue. "We'll do what needs to be done."

And they did. When Vilas pushed deep into her cunt, Rafe withdrew almost all the way from her backside, making space for him. Then they reversed roles. Vilas played with her tits all the time, tugging on the chain, making her squeal when he lifted his head and took gentle bites of her fleshy breasts. Rafe spanked her butt each time he thrust into it, breathing heavily, telling her all the time that he loved her. Damn it, she wished he wouldn't keep saying that. This time tomorrow he'd be angry and bewildered by her abandonment of them. He certainly wouldn't be entertaining any loving thoughts toward her.

"It feels incredible," she said, struggling not to move in case she threw their rhythm out.

"No arguments there," Vilas agreed. "You're well worth waiting for, babe."

Oh, Vilas!

"Let's pick this up a bit," Rafe said, thrusting a little harder.

Chantal screamed. "I can't...I can't hold it." She threw her head back, eyes tightly closed as she desperately tried to delay the moment. "It's no good. I need to come."

"Come for us then, babe," Rafe ordered. "Let it go."

They upped the tempo and Chantal shattered. Her body pulsated with the tingling, incandescent fire that burned deep within her core. It spread and her orgasm hit like a tornado, destroying everything that stood in its path, including her heart. Heat radiated from every pore and she forgot all about keeping still. She rode the guys' cocks like they were bucking broncos and she an inexperienced rider determined not to fall off. On and on it seemed to go, cresting, waning, and then cresting yet again, reaching near impossible heights.

"Oh, God!" she cried. "I think I just died."

"That's because we're loving you like you deserve to be loved," Rafe said, sounding so proud, so full of love, that she wanted to weep with regret.

It was over. She'd finally stopped pulsating, but her head still spun from the strength of the physical alchemy between them. Tears seeped from her eyes, but before they could take hold she felt the boys increase their pace and their cocks swell thick and hot inside her.

"Hell, I'm going to come again," she said, hardly able to believe it.

"Let's hit it together," Rafe said through what sounded like gritted teeth.

"I'm gonna come right now!" Vilas groaned.

She felt both of them pouring their sperm into her at the same moment. It was enough to reignite her orgasm, which this time sent piquant thrills tumbling through her more slowly, but equally powerfully. She had no idea that her body could be so responsive, or that it could tolerate so much pleasure without combusting. The potency of the love she felt for these two gorgeous alphas had to explain her extreme reaction.

They collapsed in a tangle of sweaty limbs, laughing and kissing as they regained their breath. Someone helped her out of the leather harness and removed the nipple clamps. Someone else went to the bathroom, fetched a cloth, and cleaned her up. Then strong arms lifted her and placed her between crisp cotton sheets, pulling the covers over her. Two large bodies surrounded her, whispering loving words as she settled her head on a broad chest and an arm from the opposite side fell possessively across her body.

I'll remember this night for the rest of my life, was her final thought before her eyelids drooped and she drifted into an exhausted yet very comfortable sleep.

Chapter Twelve

Chantal had no idea what the time was when she woke but figured it had to be late. She was in bed alone, the sheets on either side of her cool to the touch. She still felt drowsy and pleasantly sore. Renewed desire ripped through her as she recalled their activities of the previous day, and she was surprised the guys hadn't woken her for a repeat performance. Surprised and a little disappointed, if she was being totally honest with herself. They were being considerate, she supposed, by letting her to sleep in. Despondency tore her heart to shreds when she recalled that they'd never get another chance to wake her in the way she'd most like to be woken.

She stretched her arms above her head, trying not to think about this being her last morning in the colony. She'd only been here for two days but had never felt more at home anywhere in her entire adult life. It was as though everything she'd done before coming to Impulse had been marking time until she got here. But now, having found the place where she belonged, she would have to leave it again. Not only that, but she'd somehow have to ensure that Rafe and Vilas didn't suspect anything until she was far enough away for it not to matter. Their telepathic powers only worked at relatively short range. Once she was north of Tampa she wouldn't have to block them because they wouldn't be able to reach across the distance that separated them and lock into her mind.

"Hey, sleepyhead."

Chantal swiveled toward the door and saw her two men standing there, both wearing nothing but cut-off shorts and glamorous smiles. She wanted to ask how they knew she was awake but, of course, that would have been a dumb question. They looked so devastating that she wanted to weep with regret. Instead she rubbed the sleep from her eyes and plastered a smile on her face.

"I must have overslept," she said.

"Well, it is gone noon." Vilas blew her a kiss. "But that doesn't mean much round these parts."

"I haven't exactly pulled my weight so far, but I'll get up right away. I'm sure there's stuff I can do to help." She managed another brief smile. "I *am* supposed to work here, remember?"

"Stay right where you are," Rafe ordered.

He ducked back into the sitting room and returned with a laden tray. It was laid up with a crisp white cloth, and a single red rose sat in a bud vase to one side of it. There was coffee, scrambled eggs, smoked salmon, several types of toast, and lots of freshly squeezed juice.

"You spoil me," she said when Rafe laid the tray over her knee and placed the bud vase by the side of the bed. They sat on either side of her, encouraging her to tuck in.

"We look after our mate, is what we do," Rafe said, brushing a finger lightly down the curve of her face. "How do you feel today, sweetheart? You seem a little distracted."

She couldn't lie, at least not about the way she felt. "I feel wonderful! Stop imagining problems where none exist."

"That's a relief. We thought we might have been a bit rough with you."

"Not at all. Well, only in a good way."

"We're feeling pretty good about ourselves, too," Vilas said, chuckling.

"We're revitalized already," Rafe added.

"That's good. I'm glad I could do that much for you."

Rafe wrinkled his brow. "Chantal, what's wrong, babe?"

"Nothing." She couldn't look at them. "It's just an expression."

Chantal didn't think she could eat a thing—she was too choked with emotion to get anything past the roadblock in her throat. Somehow she managed to force a few mouthfuls down. They already suspected that something was bothering her and they'd know it for sure if she didn't eat.

"It's delicious," she said, trying to sound enthusiastic.

Vilas rubbed his face against her cheek. "So are you, darlin'."

"We have to be at the clinic all the afternoon," Rafe said. "There's a meeting of the council so we can decide which sick kids to bring here next."

Chantal widened her eyes. "You have to pick?"

"Yeah, and it ain't easy," Vilas said. "We can't help them all and Mikael doesn't want to take responsibility for choosing alone, so the council listens to the kids' histories and collectively votes on which ones they think are the worthiest cases."

She touched each of their hands. "That must be emotionally draining."

Rafe sighed. "We get through it by focusing on the positive. Whichever kids we *do* decide to help get another chance at life."

"Even so, it must be heartbreaking." It almost made Chantal's situation seem irrelevant by comparison. At least she still had her health, and no one she'd heard of had ever actually died of a broken heart, even if right now it felt as though she could be the first.

"We're running late, babe." Rafe swooped in for a kiss, as did Vilas. "Have a lazy afternoon. Go visit the shops on the other side of the bridge if you like. Get yourself something pretty to wear for us and we'll see you later."

They left her in bed, taking her half-eaten breakfast away with them. Chantal held herself together until she heard the outer door close behind them, and then wept like a baby.

"Stop being so feeble," she told herself when the tears finally dried up. "You're making a sacrifice to keep the men you love safe. End. Of. Story."

Chantal took a long shower, forcing her mind to go blank. She wouldn't put it past the guys to tune in to her, even though they'd promised not to. If they did, they'd figure out what she intended to do, come running back here, and talk her out of leaving. The problem was, they wouldn't have to try very hard. Subconsciously she was probably looking for excuses not to go, so she absolutely couldn't afford to weaken.

She dressed in jeans and a sleeveless top and threw the rest of her things into the bag she'd brought with her. It didn't take long. Then she wondered what sort of note she ought to leave for the guys. What could she possibly say to make them understand? Her gut clenched as she imagined their reaction. How could she let them down lightly?

She was still pondering on a problem that had no right answer to it when her cell phone rang. Probably Jack again. He'd already called three times since she'd been in Impulse but she hadn't answered him. Nor would she this time. She had absolutely nothing to say to him that he'd want to hear.

She glanced at the display. It wasn't Jack. She didn't recognize the number and curiosity made her take the call.

"Chantal?"

Chantal's heart lurched. She'd know that voice anywhere. "Max, is that you?"

"Yes, I'm in the hospital."

Hospital? "What? Why? What's wrong?"

"I…I don't know. I've been here for two weeks. I was found in the street and brought in, apparently. They think I was in an accident, probably hit by a car. My leg's busted up pretty bad, but that's not the worst part. I didn't know my own name, couldn't remember a damned thing."

The lions. They'd played with his memory. "But you can now?"

"Yes, all of a sudden I remember everything, right up to two weeks ago. I was off on a job…then nothing until an hour ago."

Chantal's mind went into overdrive. Something had clearly gone wrong with the lions' ability to block his memory. Unless they'd released it to drag her there. But why would they do that? Presumably because they'd heard she was mated to Rafe and Vilas. She had no idea how close the lions were and how easily they could pick up the colony's pheromones, but she had to assume they'd managed to do so.

"What hospital are you in?"

"Tampa General." He told her which ward and she scribbled the information down on a scrap of paper. "Where are you, Chantal?"

"I'm close by. Are you fit to leave there? Your leg—"

"Yeah, nothing's broken. I can walk slowly. I really want to get out of here. I need to figure out what happened to me."

No you don't. "I'll come and get you, but I can't get there until after dark."

"No problem. I can't go anywhere without you."

She cut the call then called Directory Assistance for the hospital's number. She jotted it down on the same piece of paper as Max's details and called the hospital's switchboard to ask if Max Lake was a patient there. She wasn't surprised to learn that he was. This was the trap Rafe had told her to expect. Unfortunately for the lions, she wasn't going to tell her mates about it and lead them there. Hopefully, though, they would assume that she had, and Rafe and Vilas wouldn't venture outside of Impulse until it got completely dark. She knew that because they'd told her shifting in built-up areas in daylight was simply too dangerous. The lions would know that and if, somehow, they'd listened to her conversation with Max, they'd believe the bit about her not getting there until sunset.

Forgetting all about leaving any sort of note for the guys, Chantal picked up her bag and made to leave the apartment. At the last moment she turned back and grabbed the single rose from the bedside table, a precious memento of the most wonderful two days of her life. She let herself out of the side door, barely noticing that the outside air didn't cause her lungs to seize, and got to her car without anyone seeing her. Heavy rain clouds blocked the sun—a perfect foil for her despondent mood. There would be shifters patrolling the bridge, she recalled as she fired up her engine, but the guys had told her to go shopping, so the guards would expect to see her heading that way.

* * * *

"That was a tough decision," Vilas said, sighing deeply as he and Rafe left the clinic. "It's such a shame that we can't help more kids."

"Yeah, ain't that the truth." Rafe rotated his shoulders, threw back his head, and sniffed the air. "We're gonna have a storm."

"Looks that way."

"I hope our mate's feeling more relaxed than she seemed this morning."

"And I hope we weren't too rough with her last night. I'd hate her to regret her decision to mate with us."

"No, she was adamant that she enjoyed herself." Rafe scowled. Every time he thought about Chantal his spine prickled with unease. "But something's got her distracted."

"I missed her like hell this afternoon," Vilas admitted. "I was tempted to tune into her thoughts, just because it would have made me feel closer to her. Then I remembered that we'd promised to give her some privacy."

"She needs time to get used to the changes in her life without us messing with her head." Rafe shrugged. "She's had a lot to take in."

"True." Vilas grinned. "Don't know about you, buddy, but I feel stronger already."

"Hmm, my power's increased as well. No question."

"Even so, I guess we ought to fuck her every day, just to make sure."

"I'm with you there." Rafe slapped Vilas's shoulder. "It wouldn't do to take chances."

Laughing, they bounded up the stairs to the apartment.

"We're back, babe."

"She's not here," Vilas said, peering out of the window to the parking lot below. "Her car's gone. She must have taken to the shops, like we suggested."

Rafe's uneasiness grew. He went into the bedroom where she kept her stuff, his danger antennae on high alert. Every instinct in his body rattled a warning, and it was all he could do to cross the threshold of the room. When he forced himself to do so, the air left his lungs in an extravagant whoosh and it felt as though his heart hit the floor.

The closet doors hung open. The clothes rail was empty.

"She's gone," he said bleakly.

"Don't be stupid," Vilas said, striding through the door. "She'll be back. She...oh shit!"

Rafe shook his head. "Why? Why would she take off like this? I thought she really cared for us."

"Me, too."

Vilas threw back his head and howled. Rafe felt his pain all the way to his souls—both of them. He and Vilas dropped to the side of the bed, holding their heads in their hands. The physical ache that Rafe felt was beyond excruciating. He *knew* she was the one for them, knew it with a certainty that didn't leave an inch of room for doubt. She knew it, too. He was sure of that. So why?

"She's blocking us," Rafe said, slapping his thigh when he was unable to tune into her mind. "So I guess that tells us all we need to know. She's decided that she made a mistake."

"Can't take living with shifters, you mean?" Rafe nodded. "We should have waited longer. Given her more time to get used to us and the way things are here."

"She was the one that wanted to rush into it," Rafe reminded Vilas. "We tried to make sure she meant it."

"Perhaps we were thinking with brains situated south of our heads," Vilas suggested.

"I just wish I knew what—" Rafe's gaze fell on a piece of paper sitting on the bedside table. The moment he picked it up, alarm bells rang. There was a phone number on it, which he called and then hung up.

"Shit, come on!"

"What is it?" Vilas asked.

"A phone number that turns out to be Tampa General." Rafe's thought process went into overdrive. "I'm betting that's where her brother is. He must have called her and she's gone running straight to him."

"Straight into a trap, more like."

"You know how she is about Max. She probably thinks the risk's worth it, if she's thinking at all, that is."

"So she didn't leave us then," Vilas said.

"She didn't need to take all her clothes to go get her brother," Rafe said grimly. "Besides, if she didn't want to keep us out of this then she wouldn't be blocking us."

Vilas's moment of optimism faded. "That's it then."

"We'll go after her, but we'll have to call the council together and get this place covered first."

"You think the lions will be lurking around here or the hospital?"

"Both, but the majority of them will be here, hoping we'll go off after our mate without securing our territory first. It's the land they want, after all."

Rafe sent out a code-one pheromone and the council members materialized at the apartment within minutes. Rafe outlined the situation, neglecting to mention that Chantal had actually walked out on them. Even if he told them, he knew the rest of the colony would still go after her if he asked them to. But he wasn't ready to proclaim their failure with Chantal quite yet.

Vadim, the jaguar in charge of Impulse's security, suggested a deployment of men to protect their patch, leaving Rafe, Vilas, and four others to go after Chantal.

"I'll come with you," Mikael said, "just in case I'm required in my professional capacity."

"Not a good idea," Rafe said. "You're too valuable here to be risked."

"Let him come," Vilas said. "He's not usually wrong about being needed."

With such sobering thoughts echoing through their heads, the party of seven loaded themselves into two trucks and hit the interstate.

* * * *

Never had Chantal regretted her lack of a GPS more. She took the wrong exit off the interstate and became comprehensively lost in a maze of confusing backstreets and one-ways. She felt hot all over as traffic sped past in all directions, everyone except her seeming to know where they were actually going. At one stage she stopped and asked directions at a gas station, but still couldn't find her way. Trying to navigate when she was blinded by her own tears half the time made her a danger to herself and other road users. Constantly trying to block her thoughts from Rafe and Vilas required total concentration and gave her a headache.

It took her three hours to complete a journey that shouldn't have taken more than an hour. When she pulled into the hospital's parking lot it was totally full and she had to go to the overspill across the road on a dimly lit patch of ground.

"Great," she muttered. "Just great."

She made a dash across the street, too impatient to wait for the signal to change, dodging in and out of fast-moving cars. Several horns were sounded at her. She ignored them and the rude gestures she saw waved from lowered windows.

"You got a death wish, lady?" one driver shouted as he slammed on his breaks to avoid hitting her.

Probably.

She made it to the main doors without causing an accident, but by then daylight was fading. She was running out of time fast. Endless corridors seemed to open up in front of her before she found her way to Max's ward. He was sitting up in bed, looking as handsome as always, except for his anxious expression. Chantal threw herself at him and they hugged tightly.

"I've been going out of my mind with worry," she said, holding his face between both her hands and examining it closely.

"Sorry, sis." He shrugged, looking tired and frustrated. "I have absolutely no idea what happened."

Chantal knew precisely what had happened, but there was no time for explanations—not now, perhaps not ever. He'd never believe her anyway.

"How's your leg?" She glanced down at it, but it was bandaged from knee to ankle, so she couldn't judge how much damage he'd done. "Can you walk on it?"

"Yeah, the stitches came out yesterday. It's stiff, but no bones broken, apparently. The surgeon said he'd never seen an injury quite like it."

I'll just bet he hasn't.

"Look, Max, are you feeling up to getting out of here right now?"

"Absolutely, but...er, there's the small matter of my bill."

"Oh, I suppose you didn't have anything with you when they found you. Otherwise, they would have known who you were and I would have been contacted."

"Yeah, that's what's so damned odd. Me and my wallet are never separated." Max shook his head. "The police theory is that I was hit by a car and the first person to find me, instead of calling 911, relieved me of my valuables instead."

"Welcome to today's caring world." *No, don't think about Impulse and the good they're doing there.*

"Why don't you get dressed? I'll go and find the office and handle all the paperwork."

"Sounds like a plan." He grinned at her, a modicum of his old self appearing through his confusion. "Quite a role reversal, sis, you looking out for me."

"I'll be right back."

She wasn't, of course. There were a dozen forms to sign and eye-watering bills to settle. Chantal prayed that her overstretched credit card would take the strain. Fortunately it did, and almost an hour later she and Max were free to leave. The female half of the nursing staff seemed keen to say protracted good-byes to their handsome patient. Nothing new there. Max had turned heads with his good looks, laid-back attitude, and old-fashioned charm for as long as Chantal could remember. Countless women had pursued him over the years, but so far none had been able to tie him down permanently.

"Where are you parked?" Max asked as they finally stepped outside. Heavy raindrops fell on their heads and thunder rumbled in the distance. "We need to get to a hotel and I need to make some calls. Find my car and see if I can figure out who I was with and what happened to me."

No, you don't, Max. We need to get out of here in one piece. "Damn, it's dark," she said.

"Not afraid of the dark are you?" Max teased.

You have no idea!

Chantal was a bundle of anxiety as she slowed her steps to match Max's awkward ones. He had a crutch the hospital had supplied him with and Chantal supported his other arm. She waited for the signal to change so they could cross this time. No way could Max play chicken with the oncoming cars in his condition. It took forever, but finally the traffic came to a halt and they made it safely across. Chantal's heart rate slowed a little as she started to think they'd actually make it. They were two paces away from being locked safely inside her car. No one could get to them once they were.

Chantal gasped as apparitions appeared like ghosts all around them. She knew very well that they weren't ghosts. They were shifters. Lion shifters. And she'd played straight into their hands by getting lost—if she did actually get lost, that is. With the sorts of mental powers these guys appeared to possess, who was to say they didn't deliberately push her off track?

Their leader stepped forward, an arrogant smile playing about his lips.

"Stay back!" Max stood in front of Chantal and waved his crutch at the man. "I'll deal with this." Then he meekly moved to stand beside Chantal again and scratched his head. "Was I just gonna do something?" he asked her, looking bewildered. "Hell if I can remember what it was. Who are these people?"

"Ah, Chantal," the guy said, his smile broadening. "We meet at last."

"You know this guy?" Max asked.

"No, I've never seen him before."

"No, but you know who we are and what we want. My name is Boscombe." He actually bowed. "Alpha lion."

"Alpha what?" Max asked.

"You haven't told him yet," Boscombe remarked.

"My sister says she doesn't know you."

"How's Rafe?"

"Who?"

"Darling, if you want to play games with me, you should have removed his mother's collar before coming here."

Involuntarily, Chantal lifted a hand to her throat. Shit, she'd forgotten to remove the diamond choker from around her neck.

Chapter Thirteen

The rain fell in torrents, bouncing off the highway like it bore it a grudge, making visibility damned near impossible, for human drivers anyway. Rafe put his panther vision to good use and maneuvered round the slow-moving traffic as though it didn't exist. Even so, progress was frustratingly slow, standing water and the volume of traffic choking the highway like a clogged artery.

"Damn it, we need to get there!" He thumped the wheel with the heel of his hand. "Every second's vital."

"It's you they want, buddy, not her," Mikael reminded him calmly from the back seat. "They won't hurt her."

"They'd fucking better not." Rafe growled. "I wanted to get there before dark and pull her out before the bastard lions got themselves organized."

"That was never an option," Vilas said, grimacing. "They've been one move ahead of us every step of the way. We didn't give them enough credit."

"Chantal caused you to take your eye off the ball, just like they intended," Mikael said.

"Looks that way," Rafe conceded. "And I thought I'd got all points covered. Just goes to show."

"What's the plan then?" Mikael asked.

"To get Chantal out in one piece," Rafe said, his chin jutting with determination. "That's all that matters."

"Er, actually it isn't," Vilas pointed out. "The colony needs you, Rafe, and so do I, if it comes to it. If you could avoid getting yourself killed or injured…again, I'd be obliged."

Rafe removed one hand from the wheel and briefly rested it on Vilas's thigh. "I'm planning on staying alive, buddy." He swore when a car cut across in front of him, forcing Rafe to hit the brakes and the truck to swerve across two lanes. "Fucking idiot!" he muttered, fighting to regain control and avoid a collision.

"We don't need to get involved in an accident," Mikael pointed out in an infuriatingly calm manner.

Rafe shot him the finger over his shoulder. "This thing with Boscombe and me has got to be sorted today, once and for all," he said with determination.

"You think he'll be there?" Mikael asked.

"I'm sure of it. He must know by now that we're mated with Chantal and that we'll come after her. He wants a pissing contest with me, has done for a while, and today he'll get his wish."

"That's what worries me," Vilas said.

Rafe managed a mirthless chuckle. "Thanks for the vote of confidence, buddy."

"He doesn't fight fair."

Rafe rolled his eyes. "Tell me something I don't know."

As they reached the hospital, thunder crashed directly overhead and the streetlights were abruptly extinguished.

"Seems we're expected," Mikael remarked drolly.

"She's here!" Vilas said urgently. "She's unblocked and she's in danger."

Rafe didn't pull into the main parking lot, sensing that she wouldn't be there. Boscombe would have made sure she parked somewhere less conspicuous. He headed to the lot on the other side of the road, sniffing the air through a crack in the window, sensing her close by.

"We're coming for you, darlin'," he pheromoned.

"Don't! They won't hurt me."

"Fucking hell!" Rafe scratched his head. "She picked up my pheromone and answered me. I had no idea she'd develop the power so quickly."

"That's probably why she was blocking us," Vilas said, grinding his jaw.

Rafe glanced in the rearview mirror and noticed Mikael nodding. "She wouldn't be your mate if she wasn't ultrasensitive," he said.

Vilas reminded vigilant, perched on the edge of his seat. Mindless of the pouring rain, he poked his head out the window to assess the situation.

"There's six of them, Rafe," he said. "Including Boscombe."

"Numbers are even then. Mikael, your job is to grab Chantal and her brother and get them back to this truck. I don't want you involved in any fighting."

"Thank you very much!"

"He's right," Vilas said. "You're more use back at the clinic. That's where you're needed."

"Let's hope he's not needed here, too."

Rafe pulled his truck to a stop next to Chantal's car. The truck with the other colony members in it pulled up alongside.

"Okay, guys," Rafe said, flexing his jaw. "It's showtime."

He opened his door and strode across the lot toward the place where Boscombe stood with Chantal. He took note of the other lions standing in a loose semicircle behind Boscombe, still in human form.

"Ah, Rafe," Boscombe said smugly. "How nice to see you again."

"The pleasure's all yours."

"You shouldn't have come," Chantal pheromoned.

"How touching," Boscombe said, a sarcastic edge to his voice. "But don't forget you're not alone, darlin', and I can hear every word you say."

"What the hell's going on here?" demanded a man who was leaning heavily on a crutch. He looked so much like Chantal that he had to be her brother.

"Take your brother to the truck," Rafe said, his eyes not leaving Boscombe. Thanks to his panther vision, he could see his adversary clearly in spite of the darkness, the rain, and the lack of street lighting. "Mikael's there."

Chantal touched his arm but Rafe barely felt the gesture. He was about to fight for the woman he loved, for the colony, for his life. It would be a fight to the death. This feud ended here, and only one of them would walk away.

"Go!" Vilas said to Chantal, his voice icily remote.

"I can't leave you."

He quirked a brow. "Really?"

"I want to help."

"You've done enough damage already."

"I didn't mean...I—"

"Just get out of here!"

Vilas gave her a little shove, which seemed to do the trick. She grabbed her brother's arm and headed for the truck, constantly glancing over her shoulder as she went.

"You and I, Boscombe," Rafe said, his tone silk on steel. "Leave the others out of it. This is between us."

"To the death?"

"Naturally," Rafe said, an icy calm enveloping him as he prepared to shift, possibly for the final time.

* * * *

"What the devil's going on, sis?" Max demanded.

Chantal was crying too hard to answer him. The coldness in Vilas's tone had shaken her to the core. He blamed her for putting Rafe's life on the line, of course, but not as much as she blamed herself. She'd tried to protect the men she loved but only succeeded in making matters ten times worse. The thought of Rafe dying thanks to her cavalier attitude caused her knees to buckle and a cold sweat to engulf her body. She crossed her arms beneath her breasts and hugged herself, unable to stop trembling. How could she have thought that she'd be able to singlehandedly outsmart the foes who'd bugged the colony for years?

Mikael came up to them and offered Max his hand.

"I'm Mikael," he said. "Come on, get in the truck. You, too, Chantal," he added, wrapping a blanket round her sopping-wet shoulders. "You don't need to see this."

She shook off his arm. "Yes, I do."

"Look, I know he's your mate, but—"

"Her mate?" Max shook his head, seeming totally perplexed. "Who are these people, Chantal? Give me your cell. I'm calling the cops."

"This is my fault, Mikael," Chantal sobbed. "I thought I was helping. I wanted to protect them, but I've just made matters worse. They weren't supposed to follow me."

"Did you really think they wouldn't?"

"I got lost. If I'd gotten here earlier, I might have been able to—"

"What's all that growling and roaring about?" Max asked, walking backward, straining his eyes to see what was going on in the pitch dark.

"It's nothing," she said, remembering her duty toward her brother. At least she could keep him safe—or try to.

"Shit!" Max tripped over something and fell heavily. "I think I've opened my leg up again."

Chantal and Mikael between them picked him up and got him back into the truck. One leg of his pants was covered in fresh blood.

"Let Mikael look at it," Chantal said. "He's a doctor."

"It's not too bad," Mikael said after a swift examination aided by the interior light in the truck. He produced bandages from his medical bag and re-dressed the leg. "Here, drink this," he said, pouring liquid into a tiny glass. "It'll help with the pain."

Max hesitated and then downed the medication in one swallow. Thirty seconds later he was sound asleep.

"Better if he doesn't see what's going on," Mikael said quietly.

"It's not possible to see anything, anyway."

Anxiety coursed through Chantal, along with a feeling of overriding guilt. Boscombe would kill Rafe, she just knew it. Rafe hadn't properly recovered from having his stomach ripped open by a bear. He shouldn't be doing this. He wouldn't be, had it not been for her. How could she have messed up so comprehensively? She slumped in her seat beside Max, leaning her arms on the open window and staring into the darkness, oblivious to the rain. All she could do was wait for Vilas to come and tell her it was all over, that Rafe was dead and that he blamed her for everything.

So he should because it was entirely her fault.

* * * *

Rafe knew Boscombe was stronger than he was physically. Rafe's powers were returning rapidly since mating with Chantal, but Boscombe still outweighed him and seemed disconcertingly confident in his ability to win. He'd wanted to square off against Rafe for months and Rafe had always known the day would come when he got his wish.

All right, he thought, as the two circled one another warily, sizing each other up, the heavy rain barely penetrating Rafe's thick pelt. He knew he couldn't beat Boscombe with brawn, but he could sure as hell outsmart a bastard lion. He was faster and lighter on his paws than Boscombe, and more cunning, too. He had one other major advantage over Boscombe in that he had something worth fighting for. Chantal—the light in his darkness, the love of his life. A life he would gladly sacrifice to keep her safe. But he couldn't think about her now, couldn't afford to wonder why she'd tried to run out on them. If he lost concentration, even for a moment, it would be fatal.

Boscombe, trying to take him by surprise, launched an attack. He reared up on his hind legs, attempting to gouge Rafe's eyes out with vicious claws. Shit, he caught Rafe on the cheek. Rafe felt blood oozing down his face, but ignored the stinging pain. He evaded the worst of the attack by spinning away, only just managing to swish his tail clear of those killer claws at the very last second when Boscombe launched himself at his haunches. Rafe was proud of his tail and didn't intend to have it ripped from his body by this loutish shifter.

"Better luck next time."

"I don't need luck." Rafe could hear the sneer in Boscombe's thoughts. *"I'm a lion and lions are king."*

You arrogant asshole, Rafe almost said. He banished the thought before it could take hold, worried that Boscombe would pick up on it.

They stalked one another again, Boscombe roaring his head off, presumably because he thought the sound would intimidate Rafe. *Think again, shit face!* Rafe needed to find a way to trick Boscombe into showing his throat so Rafe could rip it out. Boscombe would be thinking the same thing about him, Rafe was aware. Who would crack first?

Boscombe let out an earsplitting roar, far louder than his previous efforts, taking Rafe by surprise. Idiot! Even with the storm directly overhead and no one venturing out in such foul weather, surely it would have been heard? The last thing they needed was humans trying to intervene with loaded shotguns.

Boscombe's ploy distracted Rafe for one vital second. It gave his adversary the chance to move in for the kill, presumably thinking that his speed would compensate for the need to expose his throat as he leapt forward. Rafe recovered quickly and saw his chance, even if it would make him vulnerable as he sank his teeth into the soft flesh beneath Boscombe's jaw. Boscombe was too slow to realize it and Rafe clenched his jaw tight and clung on, literally for grim death.

Boscombe wouldn't give in that easily, but how would he retaliate? Rafe discovered the answer when he felt an excruciating pain rip through his entire body like a sharp sabre. It was so acute that he almost released his hold on Boscombe's jaw. But if he did that it would be the end of him. Stubbornness and thoughts of Chantal helped him to somehow keep his jaw firmly locked in place as the weakening lion thrashed his large body every which way, trying to break Rafe's hold. Mild elation trickled through his pain-ridden body when he felt Boscombe's warm blood trickle across his muzzle. He continued to withstand the pain that was ripping him in two, encouraged when he sensed Boscombe's strength gradually leaving him. His adversary's posturing roars had become pitifully weak whimpers.

Boscombe's supporters became increasingly agitated when they saw which way the battle was going. Rafe's people noticed it, too, and he was conscious of them shifting to square up to the lions. They wouldn't attack unless the lions did first. Boscombe had told them not to, but Rafe wasn't sure how disciplined they actually were. This was a matter of honor to be settled between him and Boscombe. Did his underlings understand that? Rafe prayed that they did. He absolutely didn't want anyone from the colony, especially Vilas, to get hurt. If Rafe didn't walk away from this, at least Vilas would have Chantal to help him get through his grief. Perhaps Chantal might grieve a little for him, too. Somehow the thought lent renewed strength to his abused body.

"Why?" Boscombe's thoughts were as disjointed as Rafe himself felt. *"You've just committed suicide, Landon. Is she really worth it?" "Oh yeah. Thanks for sending her. I might be dying, but she's worth dying for. Besides, I'm taking you with me."*

"Others will take my place."

"And they won't get their paws on Impulse, either."

Rafe finally released his hold on Boscombe's jaw. He was too weak to hold on any longer. If he hadn't killed Boscombe then there was nothing more he could do about it. He fell to the ground beside his old enemy, listening to his weakened thoughts as the life left the lion's body.

Then Rafe, aware of blood pouring from his own body, passed out himself.

Chapter Fourteen

Mikael leapt from the truck the moment the fighting stopped. Chantal was right behind him. The lion shifters had disappeared, taking Boscombe's body with them. Chantal barely noticed. Her gaze was focused on Rafe's lifeless form, lying in a pool of rainwater and an even bigger pool of his own blood.

"Is he alive?"

She barely got the question past her trembling lips as the others parted, giving Mikael access to Rafe.

"He's breathing, but he's lost a lot of blood. His belly wound has opened up again." Chantal could sense Mikael's unease. "I feared that might happen."

Chantal felt her tears merging with the rain that ran down her face. "There must be something you can do."

Vilas pushed her aside, his expression distraught. "Just stay away from him," he snapped. "You've done enough damage."

"We need to get him back to Impulse fast. I can't do anything for him here. He needs our rarefied atmosphere. It's his only chance."

Several pairs of hands lifted Rafe into the bed of the truck. Mikael jumped in with him, as did Chantal. Vilas shot her a dirty look, jumped behind the wheel, and fired up the engine.

"Don't hang about, Vilas," Mikael said. "It's touch-and-go."

Vilas burned rubber on the wet tarmac as he left the lot. Chantal's tears dripped onto Rafe's face, mingling with the rainwater.

"Why doesn't he shift back?" she asked Mikael, resting his adorable panther head in her lap and stroking ears matted with blood.

"He can't. He doesn't have the strength. Besides, he needs to be in panther form for me to treat him." Mikael's words were terse as he bound Rafe's gaping wound together as best he could. "He'd never withstand the pain in human form."

"The pain of your treatment?" Chantal frowned. "It hurts."

"Like hell, apparently. He's been through it once." Mikael shook his head. "God alone knows if he has the strength to stand it again. If we get him there in time, that is." He found a pouch of fresh blood, slipped a needle into Rafe's paw and set up a makeshift drip. "Hold this up high," he said to Chantal. "I need to find a way to keep him warm."

Chantal nodded, watching as Mikael covered Rafe with a blanket. He furrowed his brow as he continued to monitor his vital signs.

"He'll make it," Chantal said, desperately trying to convince herself that it was true. "I couldn't live with myself if he doesn't."

"He's got an hour, no more than that, and the journey ought to take longer in these conditions."

Thanks to Vilas's determination to save the man he loved, it didn't. He drove like a man possessed and they reached Impulse with five minutes to spare. Chantal wondered what would have happened if he'd been stopped for speeding and the cops found an injured panther in the bed of the truck. Fortunately that didn't happen. Even the traffic police seemed reluctant to venture out in such conditions.

Everyone in the colony already seemed to know what had happened, and the mood was somber when the truck pulled up outside the clinic. More hands reached in to lift Rafe down.

"Is he still alive?" Vilas asked, addressing the question to Mikael and ignoring Chantal completely.

"Just."

The Impulse atmosphere appeared to revive Rafe. He opened one eye, groaned, and closed it again.

"Bring him in here," Mikael said, leading the way into what appeared to be an operating theatre.

"He doesn't need you," Vilas said, barring the door to Chantal.

"Let her in," Mikael said in a tone that brooked no argument. "She kept him calm in the truck."

Vilas scowled and stood aside, letting her pass through the door. Mikael and his partner Philo set up a more efficient intravenous drip than the makeshift affair in the back of the truck. Rafe opened both eyes after a few moments and roared with pain.

"That's a good sign," Philo said to Chantal.

"Rafe, buddy," Mikael said. "You know what we have to do, right?"

Presumably Rafe pheromoned a response, but Chantal didn't pick up on it. The room crackled with tension. Whatever it was they were about to do, it was clearly risky. For the first time, Chantal noticed that Rochelle was there. Mikael turned to her.

"Chantal's brother's in the truck," he said. "Can you take care of him until we have more time?"

Sure."

Rochelle flashed a reassuring smile at Chantal and left the room. Chantal didn't think she deserved to be reassured. Vilas's cold treatment cut her to the quick, but she didn't blame him for the way he felt. Rafe would probably die, thanks to her.

Philo boiled something over what looked like a Bunsen burner. It filled the room with a vile odor that made Chantal's eyes water.

"Okay, buddy," Mikael said to Rafe. "Here we go."

He exposed Rafe's wound and half his insides appeared to tumble out. Chantal gasped. It would be impossible for him to survive. She was surprised he'd lasted this long. Mikael calmly held the two sides of his torn gut together, and Philo ladled the liquid he'd boiled directly onto it. Rafe's body jerked, his agonized growl gut-wrenching. Vilas smoothed Rafe's head and almost keeled over, like he shared the pain. Chantal was on emotional overload and didn't feel anything at all.

Mikael waited for the steam coming from Rafe's wound to subside and then peered at it, shaking his head.

"It hasn't completely sealed. We'll have to do it again."

"He can't stand that a second time," Vilas said, shooting a look of pure vitriol at Chantal.

"If he doesn't, he'll die," Mikael said starkly.

"Shit! Let me see if I can help him."

As Chantal watched, Vilas shifted. She'd never seen him in panther mode before and had to admit that he was beautiful. Sleek, black, and lethally exotic.

"What's he doing?" she asked Philo as Vilas placed a paw on Rafe's head.

"He's giving him some of his own power." Philo touched her hand. "He couldn't have done that if you hadn't mated with him. He wasn't strong enough before. Hold that thought."

Philo presumably intended to comfort her, but his words didn't help much. If she hadn't mated with them, Rafe wouldn't be fighting against unendurable pain and near-certain death. Chantal subconsciously fingered the collar round her neck, feeling like an outsider as two panthers—one full of life and vigor, the other barely breathing—shared some secret bonding process she knew nothing about, and never would.

"The potion seals the severed organs back together," Mikael explained. "Which is why it hurts so much. I haven't found a way to make it work at anything below boiling point yet." He sounded almost apologetic. "No one's ever had to go through the agonies twice in quick succession before either, so this is uncharted territory."

"He can do it." Chantal jutted her chin. "I refuse to let him die."

"Ready," Philo said, returning from the Bunsen burner with a new batch, so strong smelling that it made Chantal feel faint.

"Okay, last chance. Be prepared for that," he said grimly. "We can't do it three times."

He applied the potion, and Rafe's panther body literally elevated from the table. His cries of pain made Chantal's teeth rattle. She noticed that Vilas, still with his paw on Rafe's head, was doubled over with pain, too.

"He absorbed some of the pain himself," Mikael said, "to try and spare Rafe."

Chantal didn't even try to stem her tide of tears. Instead she stood anxiously by while Mikael examined Rafe's body. He looked up at her and flashed an exhausted smile.

"It's worked," he said. "I think we've saved him."

* * * *

A collective sigh of relief echoed through the room. Someone sent out a pheromone and applause could be heard from outside where all the colony had collected, waiting for news of their leader.

Vilas shifted back, pain etched in his bones. What he'd felt was only a fraction of what Rafe must have endured. How the hell he'd managed to come through it was a mystery. All he knew was that he had. He'd gotten this far, and Vilas would do whatever it took to make sure he recovered completely.

He glanced down at Rafe, who appeared to be breathing more easily. He opened his eyes slowly and groaned.

"Can you shift back, buddy?"

"Not sure I have the strength."

"You know you have to. Come on, we didn't go through all this for you to wimp out on me now."

"What's happening?" Chantal asked.

Vilas left it to Mikael to answer her. Right now, he had trouble even looking at her. She ran out on them. That was all he knew, and it was too late for her to pretend that she gave a shit about them. If there was one thing that Vilas couldn't tolerate, it was people who made promises they didn't intend to keep. There were no excuses for

Chantal's behavior. They'd offered her everything they had and it obviously wasn't enough for her. He loved her still but hated her as well. Hated her for what she'd put Rafe through. Hated her for coming into their lives at all. They'd been a damned sight better off without her, even with their depleted powers. At least their hearts hadn't been affected.

"Rafe can't stay in panther mode for long. He needs to shift back so his human body can heal, but he can't shift if he doesn't have enough strength."

"Which is why Vilas gave him some of his power."

"I would imagine so."

Vilas watched as Rafe's body trembled. His fur gradually gave way to patches of human skin, and his tail disappeared, as did his massive paws. But it was taking too long. The worse possible case would be if he got stuck in midtransition. Vilas closed his eyes and used every last ounce of his formidable willpower to help Rafe through.

"Come on, lover, you can do this."

"Shit, I'm stuck!"

"No, you're not. Come back to us. We need you."

Vilas could sense the strain on Rafe's newly healed gut. He could feel him fighting to get back to them but feared he wasn't strong enough.

"Rafe, if you don't do this right now, I'll...I'll set that little she-panther that fancied you on your tail."

Vilas heard Rafe groan and laugh simultaneously as his human form finally broke through. The entire room erupted with applause. Rafe lay flat on his back, sweating and moaning.

"Did I kill that bastard lion?" he asked.

Vilas kissed his forehead then his lips, mindless of his audience. "Yeah, you got the sucker."

"Good."

As though sensing Chantal standing just outside his line of sight, Rafe held out a hand to her. She ran to his side and grasped it in both of hers.

"How do you feel?" she asked.

"All the better for seeing you." He paused and she leaned over to kiss him. "Why did you go?"

"He needs to rest," Mikael said. "Come on, Rafe, we'll move you to a comfortable bed and give you something to make you sleep."

"Can I stay with him?"

"No," said Vilas.

"Yes," said Rafe.

"You can both stay," Mikael said. "But he needs peace and quiet," he added, glaring at Vilas.

"I can't believe it," Chantal said, staring at Rafe's stomach. "That line looks red raw, but when I think what—" Her voice caught. "You really are a miracle worker, Mikael."

"He's a butcher is what he is," Rafe said, wincing.

Chantal clutched his hand as he was wheeled into an adjoining room with a comfortable bed. Mikael and Philo settled him onto it and forced some medication into him. Moments later he was asleep.

Vilas and Chantal eyed one another from opposite sides of the bed. The silence was brittle, filled with the strength of Vilas's disapproval.

"I need to explain what I did, Vilas," she said.

"What, you need to explain why you almost got Rafe killed?" Vilas folded his arms across his chest. "This I must hear."

Mikael put his head round the door. "Your brother's asking for you, Chantal."

* * * *

Chantal had forgotten all about Max but was almost relieved for an excuse to escape the grim atmosphere of Vilas's displeasure.

"I'll be right back," she told him.

Max was in an adjoining room, deep in conversation with Rochelle. So absorbed with her, in fact, that he didn't seem to hear Chantal when she entered the room.

"Hey," she said. "How do you feel?"

"Rochelle's been taking good care of me."

Chantal laughed, something she'd thought she'd never do again. "And you should taste her cooking."

"Mikael put something foul on my leg and it already feels a lot better."

"He's a good doctor."

Chantal stayed for a while longer. Max chatted to them both but didn't once ask where he was or for an explanation about the happenings in the parking lot. Presumably someone had wiped his memory of those events, for which Chantal was grateful. He also appeared to have more than a friendly interest in Rochelle, as she did in him. Could it be? Chantal hoped so. She might have blown it with Vilas, and therefore Rafe, but if her brother found happiness in the colony, that would be cause for celebration.

"You go back to him," Rochelle said, as though sensing Chantal's impatience. "Max and I will be fine here. I'll stay with him."

"Thank you, Rochelle."

She kissed her brother's brow, tossed an abstracted smile Rochelle's way, and returned next door.

Rafe appeared to be sleeping peacefully, his breathing unlabored and even.

"Where were we?" she asked, unable to look Vilas in the eye.

"It's late," he said abruptly. "Get some sleep."

"I want to stay with you both."

"There's a couch over there."

"What about you?"

Vilas curled his upper lip. "All of a sudden, she cares."

"I never stopped caring, that's the problem."

"Just get some sleep. We'll talk in the morning, when Rafe's in the land of the living again."

"Will it be that quick?" she asked, not daring to hope.

"Oh yes. Mikael's a miracle worker, and that's a fact."

Chapter Fifteen

Anxiety, relief, and exhaustion combined to make Chantal fall into a deep sleep, something she hadn't imagined would be possible. Too many thoughts swirled through her brain, the chief of which was how to make things right with her mates. She was distracted by the sound of Boscombe's terrible roars and Rafe's agony mingling inside her head, causing her to thrash about as she waded through the treacle of her imagination, trying to stop the fight. No one took any notice of her.

The sound of muted voices brought her abruptly back to consciousness. She sat up on the couch, disorientated. As the room slowly came into focus, she remembered where she was. She glanced across the room and saw Vilas and Rafe talking together, Rafe looked pale but otherwise pretty damned good.

"How do you feel?" she asked, levering herself to her feet and crossing the room to join them both.

"No lasting damage."

Vilas harrumphed. "How many lives have you used up now, buddy?"

Chantal looked at his gut and gasped. That terrible wound was now a just a dark line. So, too, was the gash on his cheek.

"This time next week, it'll barely show," Rafe told her.

"It's amazing."

"Come on, you two," Rafe said, lowering his legs over the side of his bed and standing up with Vilas's help. "Let's go back to the apartment and get some breakfast. I'm starving."

Chantal laughed, feeling giddy with relief. It didn't matter if Vilas hated her and they didn't want to be mated with her anymore. Rafe was safe, and she didn't care about anything else.

"How can you think of food at a time like this?" she asked.

He waggled her brows at her. "It wasn't only food I had in mind."

"Now that I can believe, but I'm sure it's against doctor's orders."

"It is," Vilas said brusquely as he helped Rafe from the clinic.

They made their way home, as Chantal already thought of it, unsure if it would continue to be so. Rafe wore just a loose shirt to cover his nakedness, explaining that any clothes touching his gut right now would be too painful. He seemed perfectly at ease with her. But Vilas was just as hostile as he'd been the previous night and couldn't seem to look at her.

Rochelle had obviously been in and the table was set for breakfast, two bleeding steaks waiting for the guys, fruit and yogurt for her.

Rafe finished every scrap of his meal. Chantal barely touched hers. When it was clear that she didn't intend to eat anything else, Rafe pushed his chair back and focused a steady gaze on her face.

"Do you want us to release you, Chantal?" he asked in a flat tone.

Chantal returned his gaze, unable to interpret his expression. Is that what he wanted? Is that what he was suggesting she say, making it easier for him?

"Of course she damned well does," Vilas exploded. "Why else would she have run out on us?"

Something snapped inside Chantal at that point. She'd made the ultimate sacrifice on their behalf and Vilas seemed to think she was the bad guy. She'd endured his brooding insults last night because they were both so worried about Rafe, and because she thought she deserved them. But enough was enough. It was time to put them straight. If Vilas didn't really love her then she'd get over it, given time, but they needed to know how she felt about them, and she fully intended to tell them.

"I didn't run out on you, as you put it, Vilas."

"Really?" His scathing unconcern was almost her undoing.

"I left because I didn't want you to get hurt."

Vilas blew air through his cheeks. "Didn't want to live with two freaky cats, more like."

"Let her explain, Vilas," Rafe said, placing a hand on his buddy's arm.

"This oughta be good," Vilas muttered.

"I love you both." She spoke so sincerely from her heart that even Vilas's head shot up. He retracted the claw he'd been using to snag away at his thigh and returned his attention to her. "I figured that I'd restored your power by sleeping with you, so if I left the lions wouldn't have any way of luring you into a trap."

"Except they did," Vilas said, a fraction less animosity in his tone. "And damned near killed Rafe."

"I planned to leave while you were at the clinic. Then I got a call from Max at the hospital." She explained what had happened to her brother.

"We knew where you went," Rafe said. "You left the paper with the hospital number behind."

"Oh, I hadn't realized."

Or had she? Had she subconsciously left clues so that they'd come after her? Strange factors controlled peoples' actions in Impulse, so she couldn't be sure.

"The lions must have been close enough to pick up on your decision to leave," Rafe said.

"Which we didn't because we promised not to read your mind," Vilas added with a significant stare.

"Yes, that's what I figured. Anyway, I thought if I could get to the hospital before dark and get Max out of there, I'd be gone before the lions could organize themselves and you two would be safe."

"Oh, darlin'!" Rafe ran a hand softly down the side of her face. "You misguided little fool."

"What do you mean?"

"What he means," Vilas said, his attitude softening, "is that you were never going to outwit the lions. Their powers are phenomenal."

"I know that now," she said with a wry grin. "I got lost, which cost me hours."

"They made you go wrong," Rafe said, clutching her hand.

"Yes, I figured they probably had."

"You shouldn't have tried to walk out, even if you thought you were helping us," Vilas said. "We told you that mating was for life."

"I didn't sign anything."

"What do signatures count for in the human world?" Rafe asked.

"Check out the divorce courts if you have any doubts," Vilas added.

"We had our ceremony, and when we put our hands on your head and our collar round your neck, those actions bound you to us in a way that a mere signature never could."

"Besides, fucking us once isn't enough to restore our powers," Vilas said. "It's a work in progress."

"Oh, I didn't know that."

"We love you for what you tried to do for us, babe," Rafe said softly.

Tears leaked from Chantal's eyes. "But I nearly got you killed."

"The confrontation with Boscombe would have come sooner or later, anyway."

"But you could have been better prepared." She rested her head on Rafe's knee, careful to avoid touching his stomach. "I'm so sorry. I love you both so much. I wanted to make you safe. It didn't matter what happened to me."

Muscular arms lifted her from Rafe's lap. She looked up into Vilas's handsome face. All the antagonism had gone from his expression and he smiled tenderly at her.

"I hated you for a while there," he said. "Until I came here, one foster family after another made me promises they didn't keep." He scowled at the memory. "I can still remember how disappointed I felt when promised treats didn't materialize. That's why disloyalty is the one thing that I can't tolerate, but I shouldn't have been so quick to judge you." He rubbed his face down her cheek. "Forgive me, babe?"

"It's me that needs to ask your forgiveness."

"It's all behind us now," Rafe said. "You'll stay, of course."

She kissed each of them on the lips. "Try getting rid of me."

"Come on," Vilas said, swinging Chantal off the floor and into his arms. "Rafe needs to rest and we'll keep him company."

"Oh no, I know what you two'll end up doing. It ain't fair." He pulled a hard-done-by face. "I killed a lion for you, darlin'. Where's my reward?"

"And there was me thinking that men slayed dragons for the women they loved."

"Out of fashion," Vilas quipped. "Anyway, lions are much fiercer."

They made it to their bedroom. Rafe pulled the shirt over his head and lay down, grinning at them both.

"I don't believe it," Chantal said, pointing at his enormous erection.

"Fighting makes him randy as hell," Vilas explained.

"Everything seems to."

"But he absolutely can't fuck," Vilas said. "Mikael gave strict orders."

"Doesn't mean we can't play with him," Chantal said, taking her place in the middle of the bed. She lay on her side facing Rafe, drinking in the sight of him because she'd thought she'd never get to do so again.

Vilas's hands smoothed her ass as she bent her head and sucked Rafe's cock into her mouth. She knew Vilas would soon be inside her, exactly where she most wanted him to be. She also knew that even if she'd just been granted that most elusive gift of a vastly lengthened lifespan by mating with these two, there still wouldn't be enough days left to her to express how much she loved them both.

THE END

WWW.ZARACHASE.COM

ABOUT THE AUTHOR

Zara Chase is a British author who spends a lot of her time travelling the world. Being a gypsy provides her with ample opportunities to scope out exotic locations for her stories. She likes to involve her heroines in her erotic novels in all sorts of dangerous situations—and not only with the hunky heroes whom they encounter along the way. Murder, blackmail, kidnapping, and fraud—to name just a few of life's more common crimes—make frequent appearances in her books, adding pace and excitement to her racy stories.

Zara is an animal lover who enjoys keeping fit and is on a one-woman mission to keep the wine industry ahead of the recession.

For all titles by Zara Chase, please visit
www.bookstrand.com/zara-chase

Siren Publishing, Inc.
www.SirenPublishing.com

CPSIA information can be obtained at www.ICGtesting.com
Printed in the USA
BVOW03s1800130415

395944BV00009B/35/P